Crossing The 50 Yard Line

Michèle V. Beaudin

Tallahassee, Florida, USA

© 2007 by immiges & words press
All rights reserved.

Book design by Michèle V. Beaudin

www.immigesandwords.com
www.immiges.com

michele@immiges.com

ISBN 978-0-6151-7157-9

Library of Congress Control Number: 2007940422

Printed in the United States of America

First Edition

Author's Foreword

I started writing these vignettes when I was myself 'crossing the 50 yard line' and needed time out. The first character I worked with was 'Jackie' which was planned as a full length novel. However, my friend and Wisconsin writing buddy, Sara Hendrickson, diplomatically pointed out that my attention span may not last that many pages with the same character. She, of course, was right. Jackie was in fact the last story completed and, while I knew what the story line would be, I kept procrastinating, writing and editing new stories and never completing Jackie until a deadline was set for publication.

I realize not everyone sees their fiftieth birthday as an eye opener to an unplanned future. Many women sail through this without a hitch. I wrote about Barbara, Lucy and the rest, for those whose lives have been such that they come to that milestone unprepared, having accomplished all they set out to do, some staying in unsatisfying relationships for the sake of the children and wondering what else is out there. I wrote it also for others who, as they grew up, observed their elders and concluded that there did not seem to be much left to life after the half-century mark.

I tried to limit age-related medical aspects to a minimum: I have always thought that some ailments are self-fulfilling prophecies encouraged by the media that need different demographics to sell their products to. While heredity plays a role in the way a woman ages and experiences the various hormonal changes, the power of positive thinking is never as important as when you reach middle age. The misogynist, demeaning emails I receive from women my age about how weak and pathetic older women are, not to mention sagging and ugly, show me how women's consciousness needs a lot more raising now than it did in the sixties.

Some of these stories also serve to illustrate how people can modify their behavior, but don't inherently change, except perhaps in movies, on television or as a result of a brain altering trauma.

Names, places as well as many other details remain unstated within the stories as I believed they would be irrelevant to the outcome.

Maybe Betsy can't find anything good on television because she is no longer represented, except as the nagging or annoying mother/mother-in-law character. Julie succeeded in a field not so long ago restricted to men. This element of having been raised in a male-dominated society and then having to fight for her rights and equality in the workplace is not blatantly thrown at the reader, but is certainly there as a sub-text.

None of these women exist in the real world and any resemblance to anyone living or otherwise identifiable is purely coincidental. I did have an image in my head while writing about each character but it was totally conjured up from my imagination. All have bits and pieces of me, of the many friends and women I have encountered over the years and of the eternal, thinking, emotionally involved, multi tasking twenty first century women.

##

I dedicate this book to women everywhere and more specifically to all the women I have encountered during this life's journey. Many have walked along with me, some for moments, others for years, but most have made the road to being where and who I am today an easier and happier one.

Special thanks to my husband and partner, Gene Stuckey, who assisted in the final preparation of this manuscript for publication, and of course, to my three daughters, Christine, Stéphanie and Dominique who have been a source of inspiration since the day they were born.

Contents

1

LUCY

The School groups are gone. "Thank God" Lucy thinks with a sigh of relief. She looks outside and sees the last of the kids filing out of the building in a semblance of order.

The museum was buzzing all day with the sound of middle-schoolers invading room after room, talking all at the same time, none paying much attention to their guide, who now stands among the Stone Age fossils, totally exhausted.

The security guard passes by the door, looks in, smiles, tips his hat, mumbles goodnight and walks on.

Why did she take that job? She looks in the display case at the dead, catalogued rocks and bones and feels a bond between her life and the artifacts: she is a fossil; her life, or whatever they call the space and time she is moving through, is over. "I might as well be extinct." She thinks depressingly.

Lucy looks up and stares at the image reflected in the glass door of the shelves where the more valuable pieces are displayed. It is of an old woman, wearing an ill fitting dark suit, looking like she, herself, should be encased in a mold as a relic.

The bleak realization that this figure is that of her own reflection does nothing to cheer her up. She squints to focus and sees her hair, now graying at the temples but not with any distinction except for its newly found wiry texture which makes it stick out like so many pins on her scalp.

Stuffing her hands in the skirt pockets the way Karen, her daughter, does when she poses for a picture, she briefly tries to create the illusion of a younger self, one she remembers as not only more attractive, but also alive and always ready to face a new challenge. It doesn't work. It only makes the fat woman in the reflection look more wretched and pathetic-looking. Rebecca, her youngest, always says she should 'put herself together', but Lucy never quite understood what that meant.

She shrugs herself out of that pose and checks her watch. Closing time. Finally. As she walks out towards the staff office, the image continues to haunt her, bouncing back from one window to the next. She grabs her coat, waves goodnight to no one, and joins the crowd on the busy rush hour sidewalk.

She fantasizes about retrieving her car and taking off for South America or some such exotic destination, but decides against it. Instead, she just ignores the parking lot and keeps walking. There is no real reason to go home. No one would miss her, at least for a few hours, and, even so, who cares?

She spies again on her reflection in a storefront window and notices her gait is just like that of women she has been noticing lately, ones whose conversations usually center on fears of getting mugged, on-going joint treatments or the onset and curse of menopause. She shudders.

What happened? How did she not notice what was happening to her? Shoulders at chest level, chest down to her waist, neck receding from her head, hidden by an extra chin: this is what she finally saw today. It has been so long since she has felt a burst of energy for any activity that she is almost sure her imagination has tricked her into remembering feelings that were never there. Thirty years of marriage to Rob, didn't help. Over the last five years, he has grown bald and developed a hairy pot belly that makes Lucy cringe whenever he gets too close. She is his female equivalent.

She picks one of the trendier clothing stores lining the avenue and walks in. Grabbing a few pairs of jeans in various sizes she looks for the change room, trying to be as inconspicuous as she can.

She painstakingly removes her sensible shoes, then the skirt and attacks the reluctant denim. This is a no go. The first smaller sizes barely allow her feet through the pant legs. In a final attempt, her calves won't even fit in the part that is supposed to house the thighs. She sits on the bench in dismay. Even a size 14 is too tight in this millennium's idea of sizes which makes that one equivalent to a size 20 when she was a teen.

Lucy quickly puts her own clothes back on and rushes out of the store under the vacant eyes of some child sales clerk, too busy trimming her black painted nails to notice. She resolves never to go into a clothing store again.

"How long has this been going on?" She wonders. Lucy had been totally oblivious to the subtle changes which had resulted in this moment of truth.

When Rebecca's son, her first grandson, was born only six years ago, she liked to stroll around with him and have people think she was his mother. Now she looks like a grandma.

She used to rationalize that the grandma-looking grandmas had probably looked like that all their lives, so it wasn't much of a transition for them, but she hadn't. Lucy had always thought of herself as fun, enthusiastic, even slim. Looking like a grandma had never been part of her plans. And here she is, wrinkles and all, dragging her slumped back and grey hair like a tribute to time passed by, and such a short time that was.

The thought of turning 50 in a few months had also never been an issue before. "It's just a number, she would tell friends." But now, the idea that there may be another 50 years to go and those years would have to be lived in this body, with the person she had discovered in the museum glass and seen undressed in the dressing room mirror, was not something to look forward to.

She crosses the bridge which spans the narrow Milwaukee River and wonders what she would do if she lived in a city where bridges amount to something.

Here, you can jump, but the odds are you would just get wet and cold. Like herself and what is now her life, that river is of no consequence. She can just see the headline: "Woman jumps off the Wisconsin Avenue bridge." With the story telling the readers how she was brought to the local mental health ward for observation.

"I really don't need that." she thinks, imagining her family getting together to talk about what was wrong with her and trying to patronize her into pretending to be happy again, so they could go on with their busy, productive lives.

She continues walking down toward the lake, ignoring the cool eastern wind which is invading the city with its damp, clammy April chill. The war memorial museum is closed and the traffic is surprisingly light for this time of day.

No roller skaters on the paths today, only the more fanatical joggers, whom Lucy feels look patronizingly at the old lady bulging under the layers of a work suit under an out-of-style woollen overcoat.

She suddenly realizes that her feet hurt and that she will inevitably have to walk back up. The thought demoralizes her. Not so long ago, she could easily climb up this hill, but not today, perhaps never again.

She stops abruptly, a disoriented Alzheimer's patient looking for someone to tell her which way to go, fighting the tears now swelling up from a place where she hadn't been in a long time.

##

Lucy leans on what could be a window, but is in fact a square carved into the wall surrounding the rooftop. She can see the Atlas Mountains. Their graceful shadows float on the horizons like so many oases in the midst of a sand storm. She often comes on the roof at this time of day to spy on those coming home from the arid fields or carrying provisions for dinner.

How did I get here? She wonders. Then she knows. What brought her here is, in part, a whirlwind of fear and determination mixed with a huge amount of desperation, but mostly a helpless sensation that there was nothing else to do.

The months spent at the museum, and then trying to write, paint or volunteer for the senior center, nothing had worked. Her half century birthday had come and gone, celebrated with cakes and presents, but then, watching old folks get excited over bingo, further contributed to her nagging depression.

Lucy had to escape. She perceived going away as the only door to a future. But how does one run from family responsibilities, accumulated and nurtured for years, ones that still demand rights and attention? How does one leave without tearing everyone's heart out? Even if you are a useless accessory to their lives you are still one which had been an integral part of them for so long. Besides, where does one go?

##

The once peach colored clouds slowly turn dull gray and amble aimlessly from peak to peak, the mountain range now a two dimensional charcoal drawing against the declining sky.

A staircase built on a lower roof down the street and leading up to nowhere draws Lucy's attention. Is this where it all ends? Is she now on the top landing of her life, facing an empty space?

Still leaning on the ledge of the would-be window, she relives the months of searching that brought her to this continent, the goodbyes, the new life and the fears.

##

Running away had become the focus of her existence. She had told no one. No one suspected. The loneliness was becoming more difficult to bear as her family wished to surround themselves with her presence, emptying her soul while oblivious to her pain.

Was this what life was all about? Did one raise a family to be so integrated in its history as to be like the old piano in the living room? "I don't care if we don't use it anymore," Rebecca used to say, "that piano has to stay or move over my dead body." The old piano. That's what Lucy had become.

No more. No less. No longer useful, but necessary to fuel the family flame. How does one stop being nothing? How does one get a personality back, one that differs from the expected patterns carefully carved out over the years?

No one had noticed that the old piano was so out of tune that some notes were muted; or that the ivory, worn by bony fingers, fingers of fat, small, large, crippled fingers, appeared shredded in spots. They all loved the piano; no one even tried to play it anymore. Lucy had sat on the old bench more than once, feeling one with the instrument, wanting to merge herself into its polished wood.

She did not sit there anymore. She had vowed on that afternoon by the lake, to keep moving. Staying still would only turn her into stone. Like Lot's wife, there was no looking back.

One evening in September, Lucy found herself sitting in a row of noisy thin wooden chairs in the middle of a local book store, listening to someone who, unlike herself, had made something out of her life. Lucy had come at a friend's insistence, not even knowing what the lecture was about, only to keep from melting into her domestic spirit.

Her head, bent in resignation and her brain passive from failure were suddenly stirred by the author's voice.

At first she didn't understand what had provoked this sudden urge to listen, and then she knew: The woman was describing a rescue mission in South America where she had found a wealth of information for her book.

The writer's body language, mixed with her strong enthusiasm for her subject, was so strong, Lucy could feel an electrical charge emanating from the woman's aura and bombarding her numbed brain. She shivered, allowing herself be carried into the wave of words with a sense of joy that filled her mind like nothing had for a very long time.

Later when the assembled crowd lined-up for the traditional book signing and chat, Lucy approached the woman and demanded to know more. "You have to tell me," she said, "just tell me, please."

Sensing a kind of desperation and also strangely moved by this urgent request, the author unknowingly started Lucy on the path which led her onto this clay roof today, wondering how cold the Sahara would get in January.

She remembers now how quickly she had discovered a way out and the way she had managed to smooth out the objections brought up by the family.

##

LUCY

O'Hare was its very efficient self that day when Lucy, dressed in khaki pants and loose shirt, hair freshly cut and permed, flanked by a mob of family and friends who made the trip to see her off, was holding court in the departure area where fast food and security check were the only links between this world and the next.

She wished they would leave so she could have a few minutes at least to put her mind in the right frame for the trip. She wished she had one more moment alone with her husband, just to be sure he would miss her and was comfortable with her decision. But everyone insisted on staying until the last minute. The gate was but a few feet from security. It was all so phony, she thought.

The kids looked supportive but resented her leaving; her husband had not yet come to the realization that she was leaving for a year; the friends, well, the friends were just there to see the whole scenario unfold and report back to those who couldn't be there.

"I'm being unfair", she thought at the time, while trying to concentrate on what was being said around her.

The main topic of conversation centered on addresses. "Do you have mine? Did you give me yours?" and she only longed to be on her way.

Danielle, her two year old grand daughter, dressed in a white t-shirt and pink shorts, sat at the edge of her seat, looking pensive. Lucy wished she could take her on this adventure. She felt she was letting her down. Jon Jr. her grandson was running amok, causing as much raucous as he could get away with in an airport.

The boarding call finally sounded overhead and Lucy had quickly kissed and hugged everyone, almost running through security, forgetting to put her hand luggage through the scanning machine and having to pass through it again.

Sitting in a window seat, there was no panoramic view but the shiny gray metal of the wing. She could now relax, close her eyes and see her life fade behind her. She never slept in planes, but this time she pretended to, so no one will disturb her silence.

Lucy had barely moved when hours later, the approach to her destination was announced in French, English and Arabic. Her heart pounded for a minute and she felt something knotting inside of her. She had secretly hoped the plane would crash so she'd never have to deal with this future.

The foreign airport was modern. From this first vantage point, there was no way Lucy could imagine that there was so much poverty once you left the modern premises.

After a brief feeling of apprehension upon landing, she experienced a sense of anti climax: this looked just like home. Clearing customs proved easier than expected. She wheeled her luggage towards the exit door and saw a sign with an arrow pointing to an adjacent desk saying: "anything to declare". She glanced at it, not sure what it meant, then at a guard, and chose to take her chances and follow the crowd through the door leading to the busy terminal.

The atmosphere was much the same as that of O'Hare, on a smaller scale and with people dressed in long garbs and head shawls or caps. Lucy hoped the representative from the agency was there to meet her, but had no idea of what the person looked like or, as a matter of fact whether it was a woman or a man. She hesitantly walked to where she could see people holding names up on cardboard sheets and looked, hoping hers was one of them.

Behind the more aggressive men vying to pick up everyone's luggage for a ride to the city, stood a man, barely 5 foot tall, perhaps more if one counted the dark mane of hair standing up straight on his head. The thin mustache outlining his upper lip made for an interesting contrast. His eyes were darting from one new arrival to the next. Lucy only saw her name because her gaze was attracted to his dangling arm, longer than it should be for his height, swinging to and fro between the other greeters, and at the end of which the cardboard hung.

She marched to where the little man stood, pushing her way through the line of people and extended her hand.

"Hi, I'm Lucy." Is all she managed to say.

"Abdullah" he said quickly.

He shook her hand, and then patted his heart, a sign of affection and respect in the local tradition. He next motioned her to where the picture of a train with an arrow pointed to a staircase, looked at the luggage and paused long enough to cause other travelers to a forced halt. He didn't hear the insults and Lucy couldn't understand them.

"This is going to be interesting," she thought at the time.

Grabbing her stuffed backpack from the rolling luggage, she started on the downstairs run while Abdullah awkwardly tried to keep up with the heavier suitcase.

She looked around at the foot of the steps. In her naivety, she had believed there would be a car waiting for her.

"Where are we going with the train?" she asked.

"To the city," said Abdullah whose English, while being a little jumpy was clear enough to be considered fluent. "No train to the desert. We have to take the night bus downtown later." He continued.

She discouragingly looked at her luggage and wondered why she brought so much stuff. Then, she remembered that there would be very little where she was going and her burden included only necessities to survive what she was told was a harsh climate. Lucy also puzzled over what he meant by night bus. It was, after all, barely eight o'clock in the morning.

They dragged her luggage into the modern train car and sat facing each other, nothing to do but stare out the window where modern buildings stood yards from where the Berber workers pitch their black tents, and four star hotels pop up amid the old medina where, she later found out, goat and sheep's heads dangle from push carts, ready to be delivered.

They arrived at the station and walked into the hot afternoon sun. Lucy looked at Abdullah for directions. "We have a lot of time before the bus leaves. If you want to go to the bus station and leave your luggage, I can show you the city."

Wondering if she had any other options, like sleeping at the Hilton which she could see at a distance, she bit her tongue and agreed to his plan.

They started walking north from the bus depot and Lucy noticed signs leading to McDonald's. What was going on? Where was she? Just before they reached another grand hotel, they veered to the west and ambled along an area which was closed to motorized traffic to form an outdoor mall, with exclusive, American and European designer shops lining the so-planned avenue.

No many words were exchanged. She, exhausted from the trip and he, obviously not knowing what to tell this strange woman, older than he had originally imagined, and more reserved than what he was used to with most Americans. She thanked God for the miles of walking she had done over the last months.

When lunchtime came, Lucy wondered how this would work out. She hasn't brought very much money of her own since her expenses were supposed to be paid. She didn't want to make the first step, hungry, but too shy and still in a daze from the long flight.

Abdullah took her to the old medina, an ancient city where the roads were more like paths, only wide enough for horses and donkeys' pull cart loads. The welcoming aroma was that of dead fish and something less definable, but definitely just as unpleasant.

He pointed to a small hole in the wall and left her standing amid various animal body parts lining the street; she seriously considered escaping the nightmarish labyrinth but rejected the thought. He finally came out with what appeared to be meat, took it to the next hole in the wall where some charcoal was burning, and an old man in a white robe waited to cook for the next customer.

When Abdullah returned, he was holding some bread presumably filled with the meat previously handed to the cook. She took it reluctantly, smiled and tried to determine what to do next. Eating seemed to be the wisest move, so she courageously bit into the bread and was pleasantly surprised by the sweet taste of the meat, which also boasted French fries as dressing. She'd have to worry about the hygiene part later.

They continued on their trek through the market, Abdullah pointing out and explaining the functions of various artifacts sold along the narrow lanes.

By four o'clock, she couldn't stand anymore and had to suggest sitting at a café to rest. The waiter was in an altercation with a patron, friends of both parties trying to hold them off. There was no more ice cream in the shop, nor were there any interesting pastries left. They settled for coffee.

Walking back to the bus depot seemed to take forever. Once there, Lucy settled down on a bench and heard Abdullah describing her new home and talking about her life in the bled, which is how, he explained, they refer to small, remote villages. The sound of his voice blended with the station's normal buzz and while her rational mind tried to concentrate on the words, her weary body only stared and bounced everything back out from her brain.

It was almost dark on this warm August night when they finally boarded the bus.

She leaned back and, as she did on the plane, pretended to fall asleep. Except this time she did. It was a dead sleep. When she woke, she was startled to see the sun come up on the horizon. Then she noticed the mountains on her right, the cliffs on the left and the dangerously close encounters with on-coming traffic.

A few minutes later, the bus glided down a hill. The road then curved sharply to the right and Lucy saw they have left the mountains and were riding on a flat trail, all sand and rock, all beige and brown, a call to peace and solitude, a hint of hardship. Eventually, pink houses, bars in their windows, appeared alongside the road and the town, looking like a sandcastle at the foot of the mountains, had Lucy's heart pounding in anticipation and fear.

"There is no mission here." She thinks to herself. There are only people who need to get their lives together so they can survive yet another year of drought. She has no clear idea of what is expected of her, but is willing to try. Anything to be here and feel at peace for the first time in years; anything to keep people back home from hating her, anything to keep herself from giving up on life.

Soon, sensing the fading daylight, she walks back to the narrow staircase leading to her new home. Each step is of a different height, some are worn down by time and rain. She slowly re-enters her new world, the metal door clanking noisily into the latch as she steps onto the dirt floor, feeling one with the earth under her feet and the planet attached to it.

The electricity will be off in an hour. She knows if she wants to write she has to do it now. The kerosene lamp still makes her feel uneasy and she dreads the thought of falling asleep with it still burning. She sits at the small plastic table by the window and opens her diary.

"I was just up on the roof looking down at the veiled women carrying water for their family's dinner.

This simple act repeated every day, sometimes twice a day, never ceases to amaze me. Why. Why do they keep doing this?

There are other places even in this country where water is plentiful. And yet, each woman will keep on carrying her burden until she dies, or until her son marries and his wife takes over. I hear my neighbor's own daughter left last year to carry another woman's burden in an even more remote village.

I see young girls, eight, nine years old, with babies tied to their backs, I watch young boys idly throwing rocks at each other or anyone else crossing their paths; young women wrapped up in sheets, spending long hours kneading the bread, cooking the food, hoping for, no, there is nothing to hope for.

I see young men sporting jeans, smoking cigarettes, shoulders and one leg leaning against the adobe wall talking to friends or just staring. I see old men in white jelabas and caps having traveled to Mecca and now moaning the Koran all day. Then there are the old women in rags begging for food or small change.

I don't understand the how's, why's and when's of this culture. The well is drying up. We'll have to dig another hundred feet. But to what use?

The well won't bring rain. The well won't bring freedom. Maybe we should build a wishing well.

But what do they wish for here? I don't understand. As much as my being here feels right, as much as I feel a sense of belonging I'm still not sure about what I am doing here.

A week after I arrived, Abdullah took me to the 'spitar', a clinic where all colors of humanity co-exist in resigned peace. I'm not sure if I can help anyone at this point, but I can try. Ramadan is coming soon, so the clinic will be busy with the faithful, too weak to fast, but insisting on doing so anyway. Then frustrated smokers will come in with various ailments, probably caused by withdrawal. What I find amazing is that even in this remote part of the world, health care is available to all... that is if the doctors ever show up when and where they are supposed to.

The rich bribe themselves into better care, but at least the poor can survive. Three times a week, I make the two mile trek to the clinic to clean and bandage children's skinned knees, teach basic hygiene and comfort women who are pregnant for the tenth time, have miscarried or those seeking answers for their infertility, fearing their husbands will leave or take on another wife. I'm trying to learn the language so I can help them understand their own worth outside their wound."

Lucy puts her pen down, looks at the time and rushes to get ready for bed before lights out. The town generator has been unreliable of late and she dreads having to finish in the dark.

The nights are cold and she knows that she can only stay warm if she sleeps before the curtain of dry cold air descends on the desert. Her heavy floor mat is ready and she slips into the thermo sleeping bag, one of the few luxuries she allowed herself to carry on this pilgrimage.

She has been leaving the shutters open to enjoy the stars and witness the first light of day, but soon she is told there may be frost and her resting time will have no shadows to dream upon.

She gazes at the starlit night; every night here is bright with a million stars. She doesn't want to learn about the constellations. "Why does everything have to have a name?"

This is her last thought as consciousness fades, her eyes closing on a barred, windowless opening in the mud wall, facing the Milky Way in its absolute mystery.

##

She looks at the letter again. Why did it have to come today? She is, now at last, able to think for herself. She is finally a person, not an adjunct to others. She may even be making a difference at the clinic. And now this. She reads it again for the third time, hoping a new meaning will emerge and set her free from pain.

"Dear mom,

I wanted to write before, but you know with work, the kids and all. Well, you know. Here's a couple of pictures of the kids. Actually, Jon Jr. is really missing you.

Yesterday he had a nightmare and when he woke up he told me he was looking for his grandma. Danielle can't even tell who the old woman is on the pictures anymore. When are you coming back?

Why did you have to do this to us at this time? Your grandchildren need you. They really feel abandoned. I know it's great for you, but did you think once that maybe we needed you here? It must be nice to think about yourself that way. Wish I could.

The other day, Jon Sr. and I had to go to an important function and his parents were away for the week. You know we can't afford a sitter. Anyway, we had to miss it and it's not really good for his career. Dad is so absent-minded these days; I don't really trust him with the kids. And that's another story. The poor man is wondering around like a lost soul on the ship of death! He can't take care of himself properly and I think he started to drink every night.

Well I guess if you have to do your own thing that's that. But know that life is more difficult for us now.

Write soon,
Love,
Rebecca"

Lucy looks at the picture: Jon Jr. is making a funny face at the camera while Danielle seriously stares at her hands. She loves these kids. Especially Danielle, the brown hair, brown eyed girl who is growing up to look just like grandma.

She knows she would remember her: they have a special relationship. Danielle just doesn't see life in a photograph, nor can she feel the connection which lives only in the present for a two year old. She is shy with the deep gaze of someone who is doing far more thinking than playing. She can't turn out like me, Lucy thinks, with as much force as to make it so just by wishing it.

Jon Jr. is all boy. Treated as such by Jon Sr., a macho father whose dark curly hair and green eyes he inherited, he never thinks much beyond the upcoming little league game or his card trading business. He is quite the negotiator for a six year old and, in this respect has Lucy worried about his future as a fellow human. He only wants his grandma in the same way his mom and dad do: for practical purposes. She regrets that thought as soon as it surfaces, but has to admit Jon Jr. is only out to have everyone do as he wishes.

She reads the letter again, still trying to feel love from her daughter, still wanting to love her. That insight into her feelings scares her so, she puts the letter down and sits still, wishing it away.

What a mess. Rebecca was right. But the mess isn't the inconvenience to the family. The mess isn't the grandchildren missing her or her husband's drinking. The mess is how she finds herself wishing she could hold on to parts of her life and dismiss some of the people who refer to themselves as her family. That is the mess she is terrified can only get messier with time, as her feelings grow in different directions.

It has been three months and Karen hasn't even written yet. She blames her mother for all the wrong decisions she makes. Lucy knows that any personal achievement she may have in this new life will be shattered by Karen who resents anyone being successful when she, herself, moves from one mistake to another.

Rob sends her Hallmark cards signed Love, Rob. So much for trying to get closer by expressing feelings in writing as she had suggested to him before she left.

She picks up the lantern from the table where days of writing and accumulated notes are scattered and is tempted to burn Rebecca's note. No, she thinks, I need it so that one day I can look at it and not feel so much hurt. She needs it to gage the level of pain she can now feel and how long it will take for it to go away.

The rain-stained mud wall stares back at her and some of the lines start dancing in front of her eyes. She notices that she is crying. She hadn't cried yet. She has in fact wondered about that: isn't one always supposed to cry when away from home?

When she opens her eyes, she notes the sun is higher than usual. She has a headache. Searching for her reading glasses, she looks at her watch and realizes it is already nine. She has no specific plans for the day, but sleeping late does not fit in with what she wishes to accomplish here.

Lucy slips out of her warm sleeping bag, shivers and takes a deep breath before removing her night clothes. The water she keeps on hand for her morning rituals is so cold, she only brushes her teeth and quickly puts on the the same clothes she had on yesterday.

She avoids her work table and makes coffee on a gas burner which is precariously perched over the butane tank. Today is her day off at the clinic.

Wondering what to do next, she looks out through the barred window, sees the daily routine of the villagers already well in progress and decides the post office will be her excuse for venturing out. Maybe a friend wrote to her. She picks us a meaningless note written to her mother some time ago, folds it into a thin blue envelope and carefully prints the address.

LUCY

Lucy walks out, crossing herds of toddlers, hands extended, begging for something she doesn't understand and probably doesn't have. She walks down to the main village street.

The post office is a small building painted white, with a limp flag hanging in front of its massive door. She opens an empty mailbox, and, disappointed, walks to the counter. The usual clerk is absent, but she smiles and greets his short, middle aged, bushy haired, rugged-looking replacement.

"I'd like to get a stamp for a letter to the United States, please" she says, more in pointing hand gestures than in words. He searches through a drawer and hands her what looks like a series of printed, poor pictures of the king.

"Where are you from in the United States?" he asks. "Near Chicago" she answers knowing it was vague enough to save her and good enough to satisfy his curiosity.

The clerk continues staring at her, as though wanting to say something. She hands him a bank note and is about to leave, when he calls her back, rattling the change she is owed. "I'm sorry, she said, I don't know where my mind is today."

He reaches over the counter, feels her forehead, squeezes her cheeks and takes her hand, which she is holding out waiting for her change. "Your mind is great. I would like to get to know you and have a relationship with you," he says.

In spite of the poor English, Lucy understands and withdraws her hand, grabs her change from him, and mutters something about having a husband and leaves.

Upset and feeling, in a way, assaulted, she rushes out and decides this is enough travel for one day.

Heading home, a group of kids are just coming out of school on lunch break. Her heart starts pounding: kids, especially boys, are always rude to her. She heard they are rude to all foreigners, but this doesn't keep her from rushing past the school.

Too late. A group of them starts throwing rocks in her direction, calling her names she doesn't understand.

Once out of reach, she practically runs home, closes and locks the door and sits at the table, waiting for her heart to slow down and her brain to calm.

A knock on the door startles her out of a trance. Her heart is still tight with panic. "Schnoo?" she asks in the traditional 'who is it' kind of fashion. Fatiha announces herself and Lucy lets her in. She smiles to herself, thinking that perhaps she is making too much of everything. After all, she has to learn so much more before being able to make a judgment on the whole culture.

They kiss once on one cheek, three times on the other and her friend comes in. Lucy had forgotten this was the day when Fatiha comes to clean her house. They both smile and Fatiha starts throwing pail after pail of water, splashing the walls and using a broom or a rag to dry them up. Years of drought have not yet prevented women from keeping a clean house. No one has heard of conserving water in this country where women carry the burden of fetching the precious resource everyday from a common well.

Lucy makes mint tea, knowing her friend will want to sit and chat for a while after work. They don't understand each other very well yet, but somehow know what is being talked about. Sometimes they laugh together, not knowing exactly why.

This day is no different. They climb to the roof to hang the laundry, then sit for an hour, drinking tea and pretending to have a conversation.

When Fatiha leaves, Lucy locks the door, smiles and walks to her stained, tiny mirror to check on her stray hair. She reaches for her wedding ring, left on the table below while Fatiha and she were doing laundry, and finds the table bare. Although her heart is beating stronger, she struggles to keep her breath controlled. "I must have put it somewhere else." She thinks.

Her three small rooms are turned inside out in less than five minutes. She has very little and all is bare and easy to search. No ring. The plastic bottle she uses to cover the toilet hole to keep insects and rodents away from the area or from crawling out had not been moved. Her thoughts reluctantly turn to her friend. Could it be that what she had thought was intelligence was simply cunning, the cunning of an animal ready to prey on whatever presents itself at the well?

She shivers and lights up the small gas heater for warmth. She isn't going to have dinner tonight. She notes that in spite of the low heat the gas hisses like an angry feline ready to pounce. She stares into the grate, trying to make sense of it and blames it on the poor quality or the ever present dust.

She sits at the table, wondering why, when she finally finds a life which she thinks is meaningful, one day, one moment, one deed, can take it all away. No, it isn't just one moment. It is a lifetime of moments that don't make sense anymore and need closure.

Lucy thinks about how she found Fatiha one morning a few days after she arrived in the village.

The weather was still warm and Lucy had gone to the well for water. She was awkward at handling the pump and this veil covered woman had helped.

They smiled at each other and met again the following day and the one after that.

As her language skills improved, Lucy discovered this was a young woman from a neighboring village who stole away from her family every day to discreetly see what was happening in the town. There was a quality about her which had attracted Lucy as soon as she met her. Whether it was the sad smile on her partly covered face or the intelligent look in her eyes she couldn't have said. There was just this bond that wanted to form between them.

At first, Fatiha taught her how to negotiate for everything, even produce and eggs at the outdoor market, then she showed her a tiny 'hannout' where such western treats as toilet paper could be found.

Although Lucy was shy and reluctant about inviting people to her house, she made an exception and Fatiha became part of her life, just as the mountains had and the routine fetching of water and food for her table.

She often found herself talking to her in English, and Fatiha rushed into her own native tongue so quickly as to forbid any coherent sentences from making any sense to Lucy. But they smiled and shared time together.

Fatiha had offered to clean Lucy's house for a few cents and she had agreed, knowing the money was all the other woman had to buy the almonds she loved so much, but were too expensive for her family to afford. She felt good about it but not in a charitable sort of way. Just as a friend who finds a way to help a friend.

Last month a pair of socks went missing.

The neighborhood kids sometimes climbed the olive tree and snuck up to her roof. She tried to keep an eye out for them. The weather was getting cold and she had no means of shopping for clothes so she couldn't afford losing any more.

Then her favorite flannel pajamas disappeared with some underwear. That had made her feel uncomfortable, but she shrugged it off as yet another prank.

Besides, her neighbors likely needed it more than she did was how she rationalized the situation. And now…

The night is falling and she is shivering uncontrollably. She tries to increase the flame on the heater and sits, staring, not knowing what to do.

Then she stands up and walks to the table where Rebecca's letter is still lying on the table amongst the scribbled debris of her life. A slice of her grandchildren's picture shows through the mess and all she sees are Danielle's eyes downcast on her hands like in a death pose.

She slumps on the floor mat that is her bed, shivering with a pain so soft, but so real, that she can sink into it and somehow derive a perverted pleasure from it.

She is numb. Her head falls back, leaning on the wall, she becomes without feelings. Her body doesn't exist in this life. It is floating above her in a virtual world where she doesn't belong. She must choose between being no one, used, but with the illusion of being alive or, or what?

The flames are low and throwing eerie shadows on the mud wall. She no longer feels the heat. She reaches over, blows out the flame and sets out to sleep.

The gas is still hissing; she can't hear it anymore. She closes her eyes.

##

Lucy wakes up with her brain pounding in her head as if looking for a way out. The feeling is that of a hangover. She tries to remember what happened and looks around for clues. There is a feeling of dull pain in her soul but she can't yet put a name on it.

It is morning, but the sun has yet to peak through the window and warm her cot. She shivers, then remembers the heater, that sweet sound of life being released from an innocent valve. She reaches with her foot still in the sleeping bag, and the attached butane tank topples over without any effort.

Lucy bursts into uncontrollable laughter. She laughs at herself for even imagining that she could be hurt by the gas when this house has more holes to the outside than her Florida room back in the States. She should also have known the gas was low. That's probably why the flame was so erratic last night and produced so little heat! It must have run out soon after she fell asleep.

She gets up. Energized somehow by the irony of the situation, Lucy sorts through the mess on the table and sets out to face her problems.

First, she must take it upon herself to communicate to the family what she is all about and what she expects when she returns, if she returns, and in so many words. She, at last, faces her own responsibility in never allowing anyone to find out about her as a separate human being and not just as a mother, wife and grandmother.

She is determined, now that she feels the courage to face her demons in this village, to deal with the life she will likely go back to in a few months.

Every night on her meditative visit to the rooftop, she muses on how all her life she expected everyone to know who she was, what she wanted and how she felt. She decided to put herself in their shoes rather than wait for them to put themselves into hers.

Later, by the light of the now friendly kerosene lamp, she writes long letters, giving of herself and looking for nothing in return. This time, however, she does not cater to what they want to hear; she speaks her soul and what she knows as her truth. She tells them of her dreams as a girl and how they came true because of their coming into her life. She apologizes, knowing now that she alone is to blame for becoming part of the family history instead of one of its active players.

The replies are few and vague, but she keeps writing. After all, this reprieve from quitting her life must serve her to make that final determination. Feeling sorry for herself, at this time, is not an option.

Lucy is glad that she can barely see herself in the small mirror over the table or that there are no windows to send her reflection back. She discovers, watching the beautiful, veiled women in the village, that what others see is not a face or large hips or even wiry hair, what others see is the soul that sublimates its beauty through the eyes.

Winter has now brought the house temperature to 45'F. Lucy craves at least 60'F. Even the thermo sleeping bag only seems to get damp with her heat which makes it hard to slip out of in the morning. With no hot water, grooming is becoming a huge hurdle.

Fatiha had offered to take her to the public bath, but Lucy, never one to be naked in public, feared that her ignorance would make this experience difficult. Her friend had not returned since the ring incident. She must have heard through gossips that Lucy had made a big deal of it and decided to stay away from the village.

Lucy asks Amina, one of the nurses at the spitar, to help her out. The woman laughs at her fears but agrees to accompany her to the public bath. First, she takes her to the souk where she is encouraged to purchase some caramel-looking goo, some gritty substance which Amina tells her is some sort of hair mask, and a wash cloth presumably made out of steel for dead skin removal.

Then on to he hammam, armed with the traditional apparatus: a plastic child bench to avoid sitting on the public grounds, a towel, and her new grooming supplies all neatly crammed into a large bucket.

The area where women disrobe is crowded and noisy. She shyly removes her dress and surreptitiously watches Amina so that she can imitate her movements.

She notices that many women come back from the bath wearing wet underwear.

This intrigues her and she turns to her friend to see what her next move would be. Yes, you could take your bra off, but the panties stay on.

Then, while men feed the fire under the building with wood from the outside, to keep the floor as warm as possible, they walk into what feels like a steam bath. Lucy follows Amina and lets her scrub her back until it is raw. The hair mask leaves her wiry strings of hair softer than she ever remembers it and, all in all, it is a pleasant experience. She finds out that many mothers find potential wives for their sons in those hammam. She also learns that anything of importance that happens in town is discussed here, as are gossips and well kept secrets.

##

Over the next few months, Lucy gains, not only confidence in herself but also the respect of her colleagues at the hospital. Her conscience is now clear. Her family knows more than they probably want to about her feelings and aspirations and, as the first sand storm of the spring brings the hot temperatures back, she knows she will be ready to go home come summer.

##

Lucy climbs the uneven steps to the roof. One last time. She wants to see 'her' mountains, she wants to feel the pain she will have when she remembers them. She just wants to hold on to this for one more moment.

Arms resting against the would-be window, she tries to recapture the first time she was up here, almost a year ago.

Suddenly, she hears footsteps, familiar footsteps, ones she hasn't heard in a long time. She turns and Fatiha stands at the top of the stairs, afraid to make a move which may cause rejection. Now that they could finally understand each other, they find nothing to say.

Lucy puts her arms out to her friend. Fatiha rushes over, crying, hanging on to Lucy's shirt as if she wants to blend into the cloth.

"I'm sorry" she says, "I'm sorry." Then she lets go and searches into her pocket through the slit in her worn pink jelaba, takes a few steps back and opens her palm. There lay the wedding ring. Tears start streaming down her face again. "I'm sorry" is all she can say, wanting to be forgiven before it's too late.

Lucy picks up the ring and puts it on her finger. It feels right. She holds Fatiha's hand in hers brings it up to her cheek and brushes it with her lips. She opens her arms again.

Fatiha smiles through her tears, embraces her friend for the last time and leaves. All has been said. All is forgiven.

Turning back to her mountains, Lucy finds that even in this early evening before sunset, they have lost their brilliance. All is sand and rock.

The sky, now a blur of bluish gray, just rests comfortably on the peaks. The adobe houses of the village below are no longer pink, but appear to be of a nondescript brownish rose.

The flame is gone, the fire extinguished, time to go.

Lucy looks down at the people, some whom she knows well by now, one last time. She has come to realize that their routine is more objectifying than the one she left behind. They are accessories to the arid land and Lucy knows the land will win in the end. She can no longer help. She's ready to go.

Abdullah arrives with a pull cart for her luggage and they slowly walk to the bus depot. In twelve hours she'll be back to the real world of airports and fast food. She wonders which is the 'real world', knowing by now that there may be no such thing.

The sun is setting and by the time the bus starts climbing the mountains, she has made her wish upon the first star.

##

Flying above her refuge, Lucy watches it disappear on the horizon. She closes her eyes. "Do I want to go home?" She wonders. She smiles at the thought because it no longer matters. She is going home now, she is happy, but the choice is now hers as to what happens next. Her life is now hers to own and the rest of the world can wait.

##

2

BARBARA

"How was your day, Honey?" Barbara asked as her husband Grant walked in from the garage.

"Ok, I guess." Grant replied, obviously not interested in a conversation. He was wearing a sports jacket, shirt, tie and khaki pants, all impeccably pressed in spite of the eight hours spent sitting at a desk in his office.

"I came home early and made lasagna." Barbara continued. "I figured that since it's the boys' favorite and they're both leaving tomorrow, I'd do something special."

"Sounds good," was the only response she got.

"Are you going to change before dinner or eat in your suit?"

"I'll change."

"I'll call the kids down and maybe we can have an aperitif before dinner." Barbara liked that word. 'Aperitif'. It made her feel sophisticated and tonight she wanted things to be special.

Grant climbed up the stairs to their bedroom without responding.

Barbara hoped he would pick a shirt from his dresser and not one of the freshly washed ones, still piled up on a chair waiting to be ironed.

"Oh" was all she could say when she saw her normally meticulous husband coming down to dinner wearing a wrinkled shirt. She felt badly. Sunday was laundry day and she had found it too hot to iron, putting off the job until the weather cooled, as promised, later that week. She was now guilt ridden, but couldn't think of anything to say. She knew that even if she apologized, he would dismiss her excuses and probably blame some menopause-related symptoms to fight back with, and she preferred not to hear that.

"Boys, she cried towards the stairs, dad is home, we're having dinner in a minute."

Kevin and Patrick stumbled down the stairs, still engrossed in a conversation that must have started earlier; they stopped talking as soon as they joined their parents.

"We'll have a drink before dinner, is sherry Ok?" Barbara asked excitingly, not really expecting a response. "Since you're both leaving tomorrow, I thought I'd make your favorite dinner so that," she giggled, "you'll want to come back and visit sometime."

The boys looked at their mom, smiled and sat side by side on the family room couch facing a big screen TV turned on to the weather station. Grant was watching the tube from his leather recliner as if a plot was soon to develop. Barbara carried the four glasses filled to the brim with sherry she had purchased that day at the supermarket. It had to be sweet, otherwise Grant wouldn't drink it. The boys wrinkled their noses at the unfamiliar taste.

The four of them sat, the perfect family, gathered for the last time, probably until Thanksgiving or maybe even Christmas. They all stared at the television set seemingly waiting for someone to talk, but in fact, quite used to the silence of their occasional and often accidental reunions.

Fifteen minutes passed. The commentator was now talking about the average temperatures in cities and states none of them had ever been to, but they kept on staring at the man.

"So, Kevin, you didn't tell us much about your new job up in Albany." Barbara started. "Have you made arrangements for an apartment? Do you have an address?" She continued, suddenly realizing she had no clue where her son was going, what he was going to do and how she should reach him in case of emergency. He had spent the summer lounging around the house after graduating from College and no one had questioned him about his future plans. A week ago, he had walked in stating that he had just accepted a job in Albany, New York and would be leaving before Labor Day.

"No," Kevin answered. "I'll just wing it. It's not too expensive up there, so I can live in a cheap motel until I find a place. I just got a cell phone, so I'll give you the number before I go." He then picked up a magazine from the coffee table, thus ending the dialogue. Barbara wondered where he found the money to buy a phone and live in a motel, considering he had not worked a day that she knew of in the summer. Grant must have given him money, she thought. Anything to keep his oldest son out of his hair, she thought with a bit of sadness. Neither boys had ever been close to their dad, but Grant literally avoided Kevin as much as he could get away with it.

"Are you excited to be going back to school, Patrick?" Barbara asked of her younger son, a junior at UCLA.

"I guess… I'll need some pocket money before I go, is it OK?" His father reached into his pocket and handed him five twenties without taking his eyes off the television set.

Another fifteen minutes and Barbara declared dinner ready.

They all filed to the dining room where she had set the table with a white linen tablecloth and her fine china. She brought the salad, a basket of bread and the lasagna pan on the table and they started trading dishes to fill their plate. A bottle of rosé wine, Grant's favorite, was passed around and they started eating without any further exchange of words.

"Grant," Barbara said, still attempting to make conversation, "your parents called and said they wanted to visit next weekend. Is that Ok with you?"

"I guess so." He replied.

"Maybe we can take them to the art show downtown, you know the one I was telling you about. Do you think they'd like it?"

Grant gave her a look sideways. "You know I don't like things like that." Barbara looked down at her plate and sighed.

Silence is all that was heard for the rest of the meal. Barbara wished she had thought of putting some background music for atmosphere. By the time she finished clearing the dishes, both kids were back up to their rooms and Grant had resumed his post in front of the television, now watching a documentary about some African archeological dig.

She picked up the romance novel she was currently reading and settled in the living room for a while; an hour later, she checked on the alarm system and eventually climbed the stairs to her room. Grant followed shortly after. He approached her, touched her shoulder lightly, kissed her on the cheek and they had sex. Barbara had forgotten two weeks had already passed since the last time. She fell asleep on that thought, but first making sure the clock radio was set for six.

Up at 5:30, she crept out of the house with her dog Bully. The dog had been named by the boys, partially because of half of his heritage, but mostly because the animal had a domineering streak to it and no one could control its gruff behavior, not that anyone had ever tried. It was pitched black outside; Barbara tried to remember a workday morning when she didn't get up before dawn.

She turned her flashlight on and started walking towards a path along the river that weaved its way through their neighborhood. Their home was close enough to the city, but built on two acres in a country-like setting.

A few months ago, she had met a neighbor, an early bird like her, also walking her dog on the trail. Liz and Barbara's morning friendship had started out with idle chats about the weather, work and family, and had eventually developed into a comfortable connection, one reserved for dawn only, and one Barbara always looked forward to. Fortunately, Blondie, Liz's golden retriever, seemed to have tamed Bully into a semblance of submission, leaving the women free to talk.

"Hey, Barb." Barbara jumped. She hadn't seen or heard her friend coming, concentrating as she was on keeping Bully from chasing some raccoon that had just crossed their path. "Hi." She responded.

"How's it going? Getting cooler everyday isn't it?" Liz continued.

"Yes, I had to put a sweater on this morning." And they started walking briskly side by side, to warm up.

"Are the boys gone yet?" Liz asked.

"They are leaving later today. It's going to be very quiet around here again. I got used to having them around all summer."

"Well, you and Grant can have the whole house to yourself." Liz said with a smile, widening her eyes and suggestively shaking her head from side to side.

Barbara blushed and a timid, faint sound came out of her, which Liz interpreted as laughter. Barbara didn't laugh very much.

"Hey, your big five O is coming up. Did you talk to Grant about the opportunity to retire?" Liz asked pointedly.

"Not yet." Barbara hesitated. "What with the boys so far away and still needing money, I'm not sure Grant will agree."

"I thought you said Kevin got a job... besides, who cares?" Her friend said. "It's your life and from what you told me, Grant makes more than enough for both of you. Patrick can get a job and pay for some of his expenses. Barbara, I've only known you a short time, but I know you can't last very long working for Family and Children's. You'll have a nervous breakdown."

The women paused to look at the white light of dawn slowly creeping on the horizon.

"Really, Barb, you could find something else to do. Something fun. Something that wouldn't involve such a huge emotional investment. You've been a social worker for what, fifteen, twenty years?"

"More like twenty five." Barbara said softly, hunching her back a little, as if other people's burden had just been piling up on her shoulders.

"Not many last that long, Liz continued, especially now with so many new rules, budget cuts and all."

"I don't know. I'll talk to Grant about it next week; his parents are visiting for the weekend, so I'll wait until they leave. He doesn't like discussions and, to be honest, I don't think he listens much when I talk." Barbara had said that trying to sound like a typical woman telling a typical male-not-listening comment, but there was a note of sadness in her voice.

The women came to a fork in the path and parted ways.

Barbara liked these occasional morning encounters, but lately Liz had been putting a lot of pressure on her to stand up to Grant and 'do her thing' as she called it. It was easy for her to say. She had no children and her husband always went along with her hare-brained business or travel ideas. Also, she was younger and didn't have to deal with the occasional hot flash and the eminent threat of old age lurking around the corner. Grant was a strong man and didn't believe in anything unless he thought of it first and, Barbara had to concede, he was usually right. Besides, she didn't really know what her 'own thing' was.

She tied the dog up to the oak tree (Grant would let him in when he left for work) and came in through the kitchen. She could hear water running in the shower, so she hurried to make breakfast for her husband before he came down. She then took a shower herself, dressed and left the house for work. Grant had recently made a comment when watching her zip-up a dress which seemed tighter than usual, something along the line of "can't you hold your breath or tuck your stomach in?" so she was skipping meals to try and lose the extra pounds accumulated over the summer.

The large black SUV he had bought for her birthday loomed in the driveway; she climbed into the driver' seat, wishing in some remote part of her brain that she could drive a Saturn or Toyota like most of her co-workers did. "It's safer" Grant had told her about the purchase, shortly after a mechanic had suggested she take her old Buick station wagon off the road.

The week went by quickly, her case load was such that the space between dawn and bed time was filled to capacity, then overflowed with cooking and cleaning responsibilities at home. Grant knew her schedule and sometimes defrosted the meat when he got home to, as he pointed out, help her out. In fact he liked his dinner at seven and couldn't see waiting another hour just because she had to work overtime. He was well paid for what he did, but his was a no-pressure Government management job and he was usually home shortly after five. However, because his income was far superior to hers, he expected and thought it only fair that his wife should take on all the domestic responsibilities.

##

"Hey, dad," Barbara exclaimed when her father-in-law walked in Saturday afternoon. "How are you?"

"Good. By the way, happy birthday," Victor said, making way for his wife to come in and joining his son in front the television where a baseball game was in progress. Father and son barely acknowledged one another, but Grant went to get his dad a beer. They sat side by side, watching the game.

"Hi mom." Donna was walking in, cake box in hand, travel bag on one shoulder and a tote bag filled with books and some knitting project on the other.

"Happy Birthday, Barbara dear. Here is a chocolate cake, just like Grant said you liked."

Barbara had hinted at a 'turtle cheese cake', but she knew her husband liked chocolate best, so that was better.

Donna put the cake on the kitchen counter, climbed up the stairs with the bag after leaving her tote next to a favorite rocking chair in the living room. Barbara returned to the stove where pots and pans were playing a cooking concerto of potatoes, peas, carrots and a roast wanting to be placed in the oven. The phone rang and her own mother was wishing her a happy birthday. "Thanks mom, yes I'll try to go and see you soon. No, the boys just left last week and I've had to work overtime almost every day. Yes, I promise. I'll call you." She hung up, sighed, and put her mind back on the roast.

A year ago, her in-laws had moved into a neighboring town about 15 miles away. They had left their home of over 50 years when their only son Grant had decided that if they were to become ill or handicapped, they were too far away for him to help. They had left friends behind and had not found their new town as welcoming as they had expected. Everyone was polite and proper, but no potential friends had surfaced yet. "Well", Donna would rationalize, "it's only for a few years anyway" thinking, and sometimes hoping, that at 82, the years left for her in this life were numbered.

Donna thought her daughter-in-law had gained weight and considered her generally dull and somewhat frumpy, but Grant seemed happy and that's what was important. She rarely saw her grandsons, who always looked out of place in the few family reunions they had had over the years. They made her feel uncomfortable, always talking about things she knew nothing about. Donna found refuge in her romance novels, and escaped her life by living vicariously through characters on the afternoon soaps.

She was now coming down the stairs, and, after assuring herself that both husband and son were comfortably taken care of, sat in the rocker and picked up a book.

Dinner came and went; Bully did his begging tour of the table and bit Donna's hand, something which was a common occurrence whenever guests were in the house. No one fussed or chastised the animal. The cake was cut and eaten, all without cheerful songs or birthday wishes. Grant gave her a new watch and the boys called her later that night to wish her a happy birthday.

By ten o'clock, everyone was in bed and Barbara's fifty first year started while everyone was asleep.

##

Barbara came into the office early on Monday to get a head start on paper work which had to be filed with the court before ten that morning. It was almost eight thirty when she heard some commotion coming from the lunchroom. Time for a coffee break she figured. She stretched, left her cubicle to pick up the finished reports from the communal printer, tossed the sheets back on her desk and followed the scent of freshly brewed coffee.

"Happy Birthday to you, Happy Birthday to you…" All her colleagues were assembled in the room and broke into the song as soon as she came in. They circled her and brought her to a table lit up by a huge cake with an innumerable number of candles burning on top of it. A turtle cheese cake. Tears came to her eyes.

They were all smiling. "We were wondering how to get you away from your desk. Great timing!" One of her colleagues said.

"Why did you do this? You didn't have to. Wow, that's so nice. Geez, how did you know it was my birthday?"

"Ah" one of the supervisors said, "we not only know it's your birthday, but we know it's an important birthday." "Yeah," said another woman, "Are you retiring today?" They all laughed. She blushed, not used to all the attention.

Later, she looked at the file that contained the details of her potential retirement and daydreamed about opening a little shop near her home, having coffee with customers, talking about children and vacations, not worrying about whether the next child assigned to you would be alive on your next visit or still living at the same address.

She got home early that afternoon. Well, early for Barbara. Grant was already home, reading the morning paper over again as he did every evening before dinner.

"Grant" she started, "You know the supervisor told me I qualify for early retirement and I was reading the stuff about it, and, you know, it sounds pretty good."

"I thought we talked about that already." He said, annoyed at being disturbed in his reading.

"No, we haven't." She was feeling stronger today. "I could work in a shop at the mall. It would be much easier for me. Maybe I could open my own shop. I'm really getting burned out at work."

"Barb," Grant put the paper down, "you know we can't afford your quitting right now. Working in a shop would mean odd hours and minimum wage. We have no money to open a shop, besides, you know nothing about business and, how would you get dinner and house-stuff done? You might have to work on weekends too and you know I don't like you're being away on weekends. Remember we decided we needed at least another hundred thousand before we could even consider retiring. Besides, if you quit, who's going to pay for you to visit your mother or even the boys? I have to concentrate on saving for our future. We just can't afford your quitting right now."

"But.." She started.

"No but's. I got you that car so you could be more efficient in your work and it's not even paid for yet. What do you want me to do, find a second job?"

"No, but..."

"Well, that's it then." He picked up his paper and continued browsing through the business section.

They had dinner and Barbara went upstairs to her room to watch sitcoms on television. She was put off by Grant's behavior, but had to admit he was right. She needed money to travel and see the kids.

The next morning she ran into Liz again and made the mistake of relating the previous night's conversation. Her friend was outraged: "I have no money, but I'll give you my credit card to visit your kids." She said in total disbelief. "I'm sorry, Barb, but can't you see? From what you said, Grant must be making near or more than six figures and you told me your house is almost all paid for. Forbidding you to quit a job that is driving you crazy is, and I'm sorry to say that, but it has to be a form of abuse."

"You're exaggerating, Liz. We have a nice house and everything we need. Grant never touched me or anything. He's a good husband and has provided well for us." Barbara was upset with her friend for judging a man she didn't even know.

"Whatever, Barb, but think about this: you have another 50 years to go. How do you want to spend them? When did you even make a decision about anything? Again, I'm sorry, it's none of my business, but I can't stand by and see you acting like a puppy dog and jumping at every word your husband says."

"I'm sorry you feel that way, Liz. Well, here's my turn. See you." And Barbara rushed through the path to reach the street and home as quickly as she could. All this talk of abuse was disturbing. She dealt with abuse all day and knew that wasn't what Grant was doing. Liz just didn't understand.

Later that morning, Barbara ran into her immediate supervisor in the parking lot and, on impulse, asked for some time off. She had a lot of vacation days to her credit and the other woman took no time to agree to her request, after making sure all her cases would be covered in her absence.

By three o'clock, Barbara wondered what had gotten into her. She had no place to go and Grant would not be pleased. He was reserving their vacation days to visit Patrick in California where an old college buddy had a house they could use for free. "Well," she thought, "what is done is done." That afternoon, she went home, determined to get her way.

She never made it past Grant's chair when the phone rang. Her mother was calling, telling her how she had fallen down the stairs, had a broken arm and needed help. Thanking the stars for fortunate coincidences but with a touch of guilt for such thought, she told Grant about the accident and made reservations for an early flight the next morning. Grant took children's responsibility towards their parents very seriously so he would never keep her from going. "I wish I had insisted that she move near us. Now we'll have to spend time and money to take care of her," was all he said.

When Barbara's plane landed, there was no one to greed her. She was an only child and always had to find her own way when it came to getting around. She found a taxi, reached her mom's house a little before four o'clock and let herself in, calling out to her. Evelyn was asleep in front of the television, arm in a sling, glasses resting on her nose, and various dishes scattered on a side table next to her.

Barbara stood around in the hallway, noticing how the wallpaper had faded since her last visit and wondering how she could wake her mother without startling her into a heart attack. She decided her best bet was to walk back outside and ring the door bell or knock on the door. She did so as quietly as she could. A minute later, Evelyn was at the door, trying to look as if she had been actively doing some chore before her daughter arrived.

"Don't you have your own key?" she asked before even attempting to do the basic family greetings. "I do, but with my bags, I couldn't find it. Must be at the bottom of my purse. Sorry, mom." From years of experience, she knew better than to tell the truth. "How are you feeling?" she continued.

"Not so well, if you want to know. My arm is itchy and I can't do anything. You want to take that stuff to the kitchen?" Evelyn said, pointing to the dirty dishes. "It takes hours with just one arm."

Barbara left her bags by the door and started cleaning out the dishes; her mom then decided she was hungry. "I really thought you'd be here this morning, so I didn't have lunch. Besides, I haven't had a decent meal since I broke my arm." She said, sounding like an abandoned child.

Barbara whipped up a salad, defrosted some chicken of dubious nature and age, boiled some potatoes and, an hour later, her bags still at the door, her travel clothes still on, she sat with her mother for an early dinner. She cut the handicapped woman's meat and settled down to her own food.

##

It was after eleven when Barbara finally settled in her room. Nothing had changed since she had left to get married over 25 years ago. Pink. Everywhere pink. She wondered why her parents never noticed that she never wore pink and, in fact, despised that color. It was thought that as a girl, pink was the color her room had to be. There were ballerinas on the wall, papered at a time when Barbara was more interested in social justice than tutus. She could never stand up to them. In fact, she thought with sadness, she could never stand up to anyone.

She went through the drawers, now filled with her mom's recently put away summer clothes. There was an eerie feeling of comfortable familiarity mixed with one of being a stranger and not actually belonging there. Thinking back over the last 25 years, her life was more a blur of tedious but demanding work which made her grateful for the simple life she found when she got home every night. There had been no exceptional events save for the birth of the boys, no trips that didn't involve visiting relatives, not even any close friends to talk about.

She remembered her best friend Joni who had dragged her into unusual paths throughout high school, and tears came to her eyes. Joni had gone to a different college and joined in whatever protests and demonstrations were going on at the time. Barbara met Grant in graduate school and it was clear that her best friend and new fiancé would never get along. So the women lost sight of each other; Barbara had heard that her friend had died of cancer last year.

She shrugged, thinking Joni probably had had more lives in her short time on earth than she, herself, could expect if she lived another hundred years. Her friend had traveled to strange lands and never married, but her work was still seen and heard on documentaries about the unusual world we live in. There was a time when Barbara had felt superior: after all, Joni couldn't even keep a man, let alone a nice house, car, family and all that other stuff. Now she wondered if her own choices had meant anything at all to anyone. If Grant had married someone else, how different would his life be? Just another woman to ignore and maybe slightly different-looking children, maybe a girl he could dress in pink. Otherwise, pretty much any woman could have filled her shoes, provided she let him control the nest.

Barbara finally fell asleep, painfully aware of having left her travel alarm clock back home. She woke up once, awakened by her own heat. It took her a minute to remember where she was. She took some deep breath to ride the wave and went back to sleep.

##

She was up at the first light of day with a strange feeling that she had missed something important. Then she remembered: her mom. She quickly threw her robe on and checked to make sure her mom was still asleep. She then found her way to the kitchen to prepare breakfast, making sure it would stay fresh for a while, waiting for Evelyn to come down. She was weary of taking a shower now. There was only one bathroom in the old bungalow, and her mom always had "to go" as soon as she woke up.

Barbara turned the television on and, cup of coffee in hand, enjoyed the bit of time she had before having to second guess her mother's wishes all day.

"When did you get up" a scruffy Evelyn asked, startling Barbara who had become engrossed in one of those daytime talk shows.

"Oh, Hi Mom, I'm so used to getting up at five thirty, I'm surprised I didn't get up earlier than six! I've made some muffins, the oat meal kinds you like so much." "I'm not sure I can eat sweets first thing in the morning. I think I'll just make myself some toast."

Barbara got up, found the bread and fed the toaster. "Would you like some eggs with that, maybe ham?"

"I wouldn't want to be any trouble." Evelyn answered. "It's been a while since I've had a hearty breakfast, that's for sure."

"Just sit down," Barbara continued, "it'll be ready in a jiffy." She busied herself while her mom took over watching the show.

The next week was spent between doctor's visits, grocery shopping, cooking, cleaning and listening to her mother complain about how the meat was too cooked or not cooked enough, how no one ever helped her and how the neighbors seem to hide from her every time she was outside.

Grant was also getting a little cranky, calling every night and asking her to come home. He even offered to fly Evelyn down to stay with them, but the older woman would not hear of it. "But mom, I have to go back to work." Barbara would say.

"I'm sure they'll understand your mother needs you." Evelyn would inevitably reply.

Torn between filial and marital duties, Barbara forgot about this being the 'time off' she had longed for only a week before.

Every night, after her mom went to bed, Barbara would sit in her old room with a book, her mother not wanting any noise in the house after nine. She would often neglect the novel and fall into a daydream or make an attempt at assessing her life, marriage and future. "No one ever asks me what I want." She tried to remember even one occasion when her opinion had been sought, heard and respected. She couldn't. "I guess," she thought, "what I'd like is to feel so strongly about something that I would do anything to get it." She couldn't.

She had liked Liz. For the first time since Joni, she had felt something stir in her. She had sensed a connection and would have liked to develop this new friendship. She had become aware of life creeping back up to the surface of her mind. But Liz's words also scared her with the implications that she may have to destroy everything she had built just to satisfy a whim. Quitting her job was not a mature thing to do and she owed it to her family to be steadfast. That was that.

##

"Hey, young lady, wait a minute." Barbara turned, and saw a man, holding a small bag, chasing her across the supermarket parking lot. He was probably close to her age, but looked quite spry, running, as it were, trying to catch up with her.

She hesitated between stopping, running away or calling for help. By the time she had decided to ignore him, he was already at her side. "I'm sorry if I startled you, you forgot one of your bags at the counter."

Barbara blushed. How stupid of her. "Well, thank you." "No problem" the man replied. "Do you need any help with those?" he continued, pointing at the numerous bags she was carrying to her car. "No, I'll be fine." He nevertheless followed her to the car and she let him set the bags down on the back seat. Her mom did not want her using the trunk: she had recently cleaned it and Barbara would surely spill something or break something if given the opportunity to use the space.

"I know that car. Are you Evelyn's daughter?" Barbara looked up, now more interested in the stranger. "Yes, I am. You know my mother?" "Yes," he extended his hand "my name is John, I own the garage down the street and your mom always drops by when there is a problem with her car." Barbara smiled. "I've been trying to convince her to get a newer car, but she won't hear of it. She says dad knew what he was doing when he bought that one fifteen years ago, and it should last her for another fifteen years." "Let's hope so." John smiled, "I'll do my best to help her keep the car. In the meantime," he continued" I think the beast is due for an oil change. Why don't you bring it in later and I'll take care of that for you?"

"I'll talk to mom about it." Barbara replied not knowing the relationship this man had with her mother and wishing to go home before Evelyn started worrying about her. "All right. Then I'll just hope to maybe see you later." John replied with a smile that sent a shiver down Barbara's back. She waved back and drove home.

Evelyn was waiting for her, anxious to have someone to share her pain with. "What took you so long" she asked. "There were long lines at the supermarket. Oh, by the way, I met this guy." Barbara hesitated. "His name is John and he says he knows you from his garage?" "That would be Hartford's. I don't think he knows what he's doing, but he's so close I can't afford going somewhere else." "He seems nice enough." Barbara continued, fishing for more information. Hearing no answer, she continued "He says you're due for an oil change and offered to do it this afternoon." Evelyn looked up at her daughter and sighed. "Yes, I guess it is due. And maybe it would be nice if you did that. I hate going to garages and such. It's just not lady-like. Your dad used to take care of all that."

Barbara assumed she herself didn't count as a lady and told her mom she would go right after lunch.

##

It was two by the time she had her mother settled in front of her favorite soap operas, and, seeing Evelyn's head nodding, she thought she'd take advantage and visit John's garage. She drove into a bay and was greeted by a young man, not much older than Patrick, who had been talking on his cell phone when she pulled in.

"Hi, I met John this morning and he told me he could do my mom's oil change this afternoon. Is he here?" she asked, her eyes looking toward the glassed in office which opened onto the bay. "It's pretty quiet this afternoon. I'm sure I can do that for you. You can wait in the office." He said pointing to the tiny room. "John should be back in a minute."

She handed him the keys to the car and deliberately walked to the room, a typical garage style décor with a dusty, metal desk, grey cloth chairs, some dated magazines on a well worn glass coffee table and an old grimy, vintage television hanging in the corner.

Barbara sat and thumbed through a year old Time Magazine, all the while keeping her peripheral vision in active search, just in case John showed up. She had finally resigned herself to the fact that he wasn't there, wondering why she even cared, when he rushed through the door. His face lit up when he saw her and he immediately extended his hand for the second time that day and held hers a second longer than required. "Hi. I'm so glad you came down. You never gave me your name and I thought I'd have to chase you all the way to Evelyn's to see you again." Barbara blushed. "I'm Barbara." He sat down next to her and she felt his leg brushing against hers for a faint moment. She blushed again.

"Well, Chris is taking care of your mom's car. Shouldn't take too long."

He stopped looking pensive.

"I just thought, normally we have coffee here, but we ran out of this morning. Why don't we go to the coffee shop nearby? It's a lot more pleasant and it will take about an hour for the car to be ready... that is unless you want me to drive you home?"

Barbara was taken aback. The choices were to be have coffee with him or have to explain to her mom why she was bringing this man home. She couldn't very well say she preferred the year old news from Time's, so she opted for the least painful option. "I don't want to be a nuisance, I can just wait here," she started, hoping he would take her up on this. "I won't hear of it. Come on. The coffee shop is just around the corner."

He touched her elbow as he was leading her out the door and she felt something like a wave rushing up to her head, embarrassed that it may be one of the age-giveaway ones, then relieved that it wasn't.

They had talked for over two hours when Barbara looked at the time and rose quickly. "Oh my God. Mom must be wondering what's happened to me. I really have to go." John took care of the check and they both walked back to the garage. Chris handed her the keys as they walked in. "Don't worry about the bill," John said, "I'll send it over to your mom later. I'm so sorry I kept you so late. I was enjoying your conversation so much, I never knew where the time went." "Thank you John," was all Barbara could say before getting on her way.

Sure enough, Evelyn was in a dark mood when she got home. "Where on earth have you been?" "I told you, mom, I went to the garage for an oil change, don't you remember?" Barbara said, hoping her mom had napped long enough to think she was gone for only an hour. Evelyn calmed down. "Sorry, I forgot. How's John?"

"He seemed fine, I guess." Barbara replied. Evelyn continued, "You know, he lost his wife a couple of years ago and can't seem to get over it. Breast cancer, was what she died of. The poor man." "Is that so?" Barbara said knowing the story full well since she and John had exchanged a lot of information, some probably more intimate than she cared to admit over those two hours. She was also painfully aware that the picture she had painted of Grant was not exactly a flattering one.

Grant was still calling every night and getting more impatient. "Grant," she thought, "was much easier to handle from afar." She never realized until now that he couldn't communicate very well over the phone. He needed a physical presence to dominate. He would mumble, complain and, failing some specific subject to be discussed, end the call. Work-wise, she had told her supervisor about the family emergency and had obtained a leave of absence until Evelyn could take care of herself. So, she settled nicely in her childhood home, waiting for a sign that would lead her to whatever her future held.

Two days later, when mother and daughter were just about to settle in front of the TV set for an evening of sitcoms, the door bell rang. Barbara looked at her mom for direction. "Well, Barbara, why are you staring at me, the door bell is ringing."

When Barbara opened the door, John was standing there, dressed in khakis and a burgundy polo which gave him a relaxed but handsome appearance. "Well," he said, "can I come in?" "Well, sure, come in" Barbara uttered in total confusion. "Mom, it's John from the garage." Evelyn looked at the man, puzzled as to why her mechanic would come to her home. "Did you forget to put a screw back on the car?" she asked. John laughed. "No. I just had told Barbara I was going to send the bill and, seeing that your house is so close to the shop, I decided to bring it over myself." "Let me get my check book." Evelyn went to rise, but John motioned her down. "You don't have to pay now. You can send it later." Having said this, he just stood on the threshold, apparently waiting for an invitation to come into the living room.

Barbara's manners took over the common sense that was telling her to just say goodbye right now and for good. "Come on in," she said, "we were just about to have tea. Would you like to join us?" "Well," he hesitated, "if it's not too much trouble and if your mother doesn't mind." He glanced at Evelyn who simply shrugged.

The conversation, with Evelyn present in the room, was not as comfortable or easy as it had been before. It centered on road-worthiness of cars, traffic violations and broken bones. At eight thirty, Evelyn rose and declared "I'm an early bird. I'm going upstairs now. Coming Barbara?" "Sure," Barbara answered, and turning to their guest, "sorry to rush you John, but it is getting late. I'll walk you to the door." Evelyn started up the stair and was soon heard turning the tap on in the washroom.

"I'm sorry" Barbara said, for no particular reason. "I understand." John smiled. "I have a mother too. Anyway, why don't you drop by the shop again this week? I'd like to make sure your mom's car is in top shape and give it a 'once-over'" Barbara hesitated. "On the house." John continued. "I just think you would feel better if you knew all was right with the car before she starts driving again." She was still speechless. "OK, let's say you bring it in Wednesday. You'll still be here, right?" "Yes, but…" "No but's. I'll see you around eleven. Maybe Chris can start on the car and we can grab a bite to eat at the coffee shop."

He turned and walked away before Barbara had a chance to reply. Or, she wondered, did she purposely adopt this attitude as tacit agreement, one which would not compromise her in any way?

Wednesday came faster than she wished and, to her own shame, she made up some story about having to go and do an errand for Grant in the city. This would give her at least two hours of freedom, time enough to enjoy lunch with John.

He was already in his office when she arrived. "Hi Barb, hope you're hungry, there is this little Italian place near by that I'm sure you'll love." His hair was freshly trimmed, his green shirt tucked into the well creased Dockers' pants, and the scent emanating from him as an aura, had to be expensive. She felt like this was a date and pangs of guilt rose up in her chest. "I'm not sure I should be going to lunch with you," she started. "Nonsense. Let's go."

He gave the car keys to his mechanic as well as some brief instructions and led her outside. She followed, glad that the decision was out of her hands, but also sad in the knowledge that it had taken him very little time to figure out that she can't stand up to anyone. She hoped he wouldn't use this to his advantage but consciously decided to enjoy the day.

No talks about spouses, illnesses or age. The conversation was light and centered on the arts, plays he had seen, movies she had liked and books they had both read. She was surprised that a mechanic would be more attuned to these intellectual pursuits than Grant who had spent most of his young adulthood in school, coming out with honor's degrees and diplomas.

Barbara was completely taken by the interest John had in everything she said and, mellowed by a glass of Chianti, talked of dreams and aspirations she hadn't thought about in years.

They walked back to the shop. Evelyn's car had been washed and was patiently waiting by the curb. Chris was nowhere in sight. John retrieved the keys from the office and opened the car door. As Barbara was making herself comfortable, he leaned over, and lightly touched her shoulder. She shivered. "Thank you, Barbara. I haven't had such an interesting conversation since..." he hesitated, "well, since I've been on my own." He brushed his lips against her head. By the time she looked up, he had closed her door and was smiling at her while walking back to the mechanics' bay. She blushed, turn the key in the ignition and left. It was after three, she had wine on her breath, but never wondered what her mom would say if she knew.

Evelyn was asleep in front of the tube, as was her habit. Barbara was glad she did not have to deal with her for now. She would probably say she had been back for a while, should her mother awaken.

Barbara went up to her room, remembering the few dates she had before meeting Grant and excitement filling her head. "What is happening to me?" she wondered. She liked the rediscovered feelings, but did not feel entirely right about them. She lied on her bed for what must have been an hour, recapping the lunch's event.

"Barbara, Barbara, are you here?" Barbara was started out of a semi-slumber into reality. "I'm upstairs, mom. I'll come right down." She passed by the washroom to brush her teeth and eliminate any remnant of wine smell or taste. She smiled: it was just like a teenage date.

"I came back early," she told her mom, "and decided to take a nap." Evelyn nodded. "I think I may have slept a bit myself. Don't know why. I don't usually." Barbara smiled. "I'll make tea and start on dinner."

The kitchen overlooked a garden which, at one time, had been filled with vegetables in the summer and snow in the winter. Now, a few wild flowers had taken over and there was an air of sterility about the brownish green lawn. "Just like me." She thought depressively. She wasn't hungry but knew she'd have to eat, if only to show her mother that yes, she had been home most of the afternoon.

Two more days. Grant was now talking about flying over to see for himself if his mother-in-law still needed her daughter. Barbara managed to talk him out of it. The thought of Grant running into John, however unlikely, was sending shivers down her spine. It just couldn't happen. She persuaded him that she would probably fly back within a week since the doctor had said her mother's cast would be replaced by one which would afford her more flexibility and allow her to take care of herself. He finally agreed but not without warning Barbara that the house was falling apart without her and that he really did not like to have her so far away from home.

By that time, she had already agreed to have dinner with John on the Saturday and was guiltily looking forward to it. She wondered if this was asking for trouble, but she shrugged: they were only friends and she saw nothing wrong with it. The story concocted for Evelyn's benefit was that she had run into an old school friend and would be having dinner at her house on that night. Barbara felt safe as she knew her mom wouldn't invite the 'friend' to her own home, since she never liked any of Barbara's acquaintances.

On Saturday, Barbara paced around the house before taking a shower and getting ready for her 'date'. Evelyn was avoiding her. Her daughter had become a source of annoyance lately and she was yearning for the peaceful loneliness of before the accident. She had forgotten how Barbara's furtiveness and bland agreeability could get on her nerves. She no longer got enjoyment out of manipulating her daughter and wished her gone.

John and Barbara had decided to meet at the restaurant, an upscale sea food establishment with servers and maitre-d's all in tuxedos. Barbara hesitated before going in, wondering if she was doing the right thing. "We're just friends, and that's it." She convinced herself of that and bravely walked into the foyer.

John was there already and motioned her to follow. They were seated by a fireplace, soft music in the background and large menus, on the table. He quickly scanned the wine list and ordered a bottle of a German sparkling wine and a light appetizer dish.

The conversation picked up where it had left off at their previous luncheon encounter, and they were soon laughing, knees occasionally brushing against each other under the white tablecloth. The food was as light and rich as the décor. Barbara hadn't seen anything like this since, well, she thought, since she had been married. She was Cinderella and John was her prince. She wondered "what if". "What if I had met him first? What if I just took off with him tonight?" Her eyes were shining with the wine's sparkles and she just sat back and enjoyed the moment.

Dessert had just been served, the coffee poured and Barbara was just about to savor the creamy éclair when John leaned over toward her. His hand reached hers; he looked into her eyes, smiled and just squeezed her fingers before going back to his own plate. Barbara was speechless. She kept her mouth filled with bits of cream to avoid the uncomfortable moment. The check came and, in spite of her offer, he handed a credit card to the server and they waited for his return in silence.

Barbara wished the wine away, although she knew she was not inebriated and that her ambiguity only stemmed from her own confused feelings. She couldn't think. All she could see was this handsome man smiling at her. John had such physical presence that even Grant's head would seem small next to his.

They left the restaurant and walked slowly to her car. She had the keys out but he kept her hand from reaching for the door. She thought John may want to open the door for her, so she allowed him to take the keys. However, he only held on to her hand, then put his arm on her shoulder and pulled her over to him. Before she could react, his lips were on hers and her legs weakened as did most of her previous determination of friendship.

A car entered the restaurant parking lot and a beam of light crossed the couple. This flash of white light was a slap on Barbara's face. She regained control, grabbed her keys back, got in the car and raced out of the lot. As she was driving back to her childhood home, she had visions of Grant alone, angry parents on both sides, hurt children, life turned upside down, no more peace or rest. She couldn't get away fast enough.

Although she realized it was well after ten, she noisily walked into the house, ran up the stairs, packed her suitcase, cleaned out the bathroom of personal effects, called the airline and a cab to the airport. "I'm sorry mom; I really have to leave now." Puzzled, but glad she didn't have to ask her daughter to leave, Evelyn didn't even ask if something urgent had come up. She could only stand in her nightgown and wait for Barbara to leave. "I'll call Grant from the airport, so he can pick me up." She knew it was too late for Grant to call here tonight and, by the time he was up tomorrow, a late riser on Sundays, she would be home already.

There were no flights that night, but she knew she couldn't spend one more minute in that house. She had come close to losing everything in one fleeting minute. She had to be gone, knowing she may never return, or at least not until Evelyn died. "She'll just have to visit us from now on," she thought to herself. The taxi arrived and after a brief hug and kiss, Barbara left her childhood home probably for the last time. She thought she saw John's car driving around the corner as she was leaving in the cab, but she'd never be sure.

##

The Holidays are coming, but it's still warm enough to sit outside and read.

Barbara's eyes rest on the garden her husband just cleaned up and prepared for next year's flower crop. She looks up at Grant and feelings of security and comfort pass through her. She no longer walks the dog on the trail. She and Bully now amble through the neighborhood; she doesn't want to see Liz anymore. Grant is all she needs for company. She may be a doormat, but now, every time she remembers her brief encounter with independence, fear causes her hands to start shaking. This is her life. This is where she belongs. More than this is too much and definitely not for Barbara.

##

3

BETSY

Elbows on the kitchen table, both hands supporting her head, Betsy glanced up at the time. The ancient wall clock showed it was past eight. She sighed. Carl was supposed to be home two hours ago.

Dinner was in the oven, overcooked and stale; Betsy looked at the salad in front of her and saw it had wilted. She wondered why she just sat there always waiting, and for what?

The phone rang. She reluctantly got up and reached for the wall phone. I should have known, she thought, hesitant to pick up the receiver.

"Hi, it's me" said Carl.

"Where are you?" What else was there to ask?

"Well, you know it's inventory time and I had to stay late to help the new people sort things out."

She had heard that or a variation of it, many times over the last few months. She knew when it was true because the store phone number showed on caller ID. This one was listed as 'private' as it had frequently been lately.

"When will you be home?"

"Oh, he hesitated, I don't know, in an hour or whatever. Don't wait up for me."

"What about dinner?" She asked, looking at the sad looking meal waiting.

"Don't worry about it. We ordered a pizza here... well gotta go... see you later." He hung up before she had a chance to respond.

Betsy took dinner out of the oven and nibbled on the dried up casserole. That was the sum of her life. To wait on her husband, cook, clean and then wait for him. She threw the whole content of the pan in the garbage, walked to the living room, sat on the well-worn couch and turned the TV on.

Surfing from one channel to another she reflected that there was rarely anything worth watching anymore. She used to enjoy television, but either it had become totally mindless or she was evolving as a viewer. Who knows? She stopped her search at some prehistoric sitcom and wondered how many of the actors on the screen were now dead. Depressing. She remembered that Carl promised her a 'special' weekend next month for her fiftieth birthday. "Maybe he'll be home that weekend," she thought sarcastically, that would certainly make it special.

Betsy's mind drifted to the children. She hadn't seen Susan, her oldest, since Christmas. Her college experience had lasted only two years and didn't serve her that well as a waitress in New York's West Village. "Why did she want to run away from here so badly?" she pondered.

Everything always seemed to be so pleasant at home: Betsy cleaned, cooked and served them with the same dedication she saw reflected on the face of the sitcom mom now busy baking cookies on the small screen. The kids would go to school, sit with her and Carl in the same pew every Sunday and then, there would be Sunday's roast beef dinner or an outdoor barbecue in the summer.

All was so nice and predictable then. She even had favorite soap operas and enjoyed them every afternoon, just before preparing dinner. Who needed more than this? What had happened to her comfortable nest?

Her thoughts moved to her son, Carl Jr. He was a different story. Built in his father's image, he had worked with him at the hardware store since graduating from high school and would defend his dad no matter what the argument was. No indication or hint of college potential for him.

One thing bothered Betsy: now that she thought of it, he was avoiding her a lot lately. She had not seen him in days and, considering that he still lived at home, this almost had to be deliberate. "He will live at home forever," she thought, felling a sense of guilt for wishing him out and, at the same time, some security in knowing he was the only predictable factor that kept her life at home together.

Girls who met this 23 year old man still living with his parents, knew that they could never hold a strong place in his life and avoided getting too serious. Tonight, he was probably hustling for extra spending money at the bowling alley. Betsy always worried that his aggressive looks combined with a macho attitude would one day get him into more trouble than he could handle.

Her eyes, roamed around the room, taking stock of the memories this space held; the house had seen each of her children grow up. She smiled at Mary Beth's high school graduation picture on the mantel. Even at 21, she was still mom's little girl.

Mary Beth was majoring in psychology at the local state college and was always home early unless, like tonight, she was staying with one of her girlfriends on campus. "She's the one who will give me grandchildren" Betsy reflects. "I must be the only 50 year old on the block with no grandchildren. Twelve years of religious education had her naively believing that her children were still virgins, waiting for the right person to magically show up.

She didn't really have a favorite, but Mary Beth always stirred something inside no one else had access to. She remembered how upset Carl had been when she got pregnant, the third time in almost as many years. Her birth marked the end of any rewarding sex life, except for drunken occasions when Carl forced himself on her. Even then, she quickly used spermicidal creams to prevent any more pregnancies and prayed afterward out of guilt and shame, listening to her husband snoring next to her.

Her life had been so predicable and rooted in a daily routine, between the children's needs and the house work, she had never noticed that she and Carl only shared the same roof. He barely acknowledged the kids, even Carl Jr. who followed him like a shadow. Tonight a door was opening in her mind; a door she wished had stayed closed. She longed for the good old days when women her age were either already dead or hoping to be within a few years.

BETSY

##

By the time the front door opened, Betsy had dozed off on the couch. She jumped up as Carl walked in, whatever graying hair he had left, disheveled, trying to be quiet, keys dangling from his sausage-like fingers. The grandfather clock chimed eleven. One look at him told her he had been drinking. His blue work shirt was half out of his pants and those were wrinkled beyond recognition. His cheeks were red and his eyes blurry.

"Where have you been?" Betsy asked, more out of habit than with any expectation of truth.

"Well, a bunch of us went for drinks after work."

"Couldn't you call?" He should at least feel guilty, she thought, holding on to her anger.

Carl shrugged and climbed up the stairs to their room. Betsy followed closely, expecting some better explanation. She picked up a sweet scent of liquor (or was it perfume?) in his track.

He went to the bathroom and slammed the door on any further explanation or discussion.

Carl never came to bed but went back downstairs to watch some late show. Betsy eventually heard her son come home, share a laugh with his dad and crawl up to his attic room. She found her husband asleep on the couch the next morning.

She prayed and tried to tell herself everything would be all right, but, at the same time, she felt an urgency to do something. The depression she was deliberately avoiding to face was consuming her. Betsy's father had died early when she was a teenager and her mom lingered just long enough to see her daughter married and settled down. Her brother had moved to the west coast with his family and they only communicated on birthdays and holidays. Betsy's family had not been as close as she wished but she could have used a mother' shoulder to cry on right now.

"Father Nelson," she thought. "I'll give him a call." As a twenty year member of the parish, she had grown to like the old man and trust his judgment, but this was the first time she would talk to him about personal problems. She gathered her courage and dialed the church's number.

Sitting in the parlor, her back aching from trying to stay erect in this old armless tapestry chair, Betsy waited for the priest. The housekeeper had let her in, barely acknowledging her presence and returned to the kitchen.

Betsy fidgeted with no magazine or distraction in sight to help calm her down. Some hymn book was lying around on a side table, but she was not in the mood for that. It had been more and more difficult for her to pray lately. She made a mental note to tell the good Father about that.

"Sorry to have kept you waiting Betsy," the tall, white haired, slightly bulging man claimed, extending his hand in greeting.

"That's OK. I have all the time in the world." These were the only words Betsy was able to blurt out, shocked to realize how true they were. She timidly and weakly shook the priest's extended hand, embarrassed, knowing her own palm to be damp and soft.

"What can I do for you?" he continued. "Are any of your wonderful children getting married? You have such a great family and we're so glad to have you as parishioners. No one is a faithful to this church as you are!

She smiled, but wondered how he had not noticed that none of the children had been in church since high school and that Carl was often missing from her side at mass. "Thank you. No, no one is getting married. I guess that would be nice. No, it's" she hesitated, "it's more personal."

"Let's go to my office and chat" father Nelson said, leading the way to the rear of the rectory with a casual gait, meant for Betsy to feel more comfortable in his wake.

They walked through a narrow, austere corridor, lined by drab, faded flowers on time-worn wallpaper, probably hung in the early fifty's.

The priest's office, by contrast, was bright with large windows facing a cheerful garden and leather bound books on mahogany shelves lining every inch of the walls.

Father Nelson motioned Betsy to sit on the small decorative velour chair in front of his desk behind which he retreated and settled in a large, impressive high winged burgundy leather seat. Betsy remained silent, wondering how fast she could run out and end this painful moment.

They exchanged observations about the weather and a potential early spring; Father Nelson, seeing that his guest was staring at the floor, reluctant to talk, jumped right in.

"So, what brings you here, Betsy?" the priest asked.

She looked up at him, lowered her eyes again, biting on her lower lip for courage.

"Betsy, I've been a priest for over 40 years. Nothing shocks me anymore and, I am your friend. Please tell me, what's wrong?"

Betsy lifted her head and saw his genuinely concerned smile, his fatherly, caring demeanor and with her eyes back staring at the floor, started talking.

"It's Carl. No, it's me. Well, I don't know. I don't think our marriage is working anymore" she started.

"What makes you say that?"

"Well, she lowered her eyes again. We've not, you know, been close for a while."

She looked up to see if he understood what she meant, but the priest was simply nodding and looking at her with the compassionate eyes he used when giving his last blessing on Sunday.

"He stays out late, three, four times a week. I think maybe he's seeing" she hesitated again, "another woman."

There, she'd said it. It felt good, but at the same time, Pandora's Box was now open and fair game for everyone to look into. She sat back in the chair and waited for a reaction, or maybe a magic word that would make it all better. There was no sign of emotion on Father Nelson's face, save for his white brows which appeared to have grown closer. She looked down again, this time playing with her fingers, mentally counting the seconds between each pause.

"How long have you been married, Betsy?" the priest asked.

"It'll be twenty five years in July."

The priest nodded his head, paused and asked:

"How old are you now Betsy?"

Betsy raised her head, wondering what her age could possibly have to do with this conversation, but was intimidated enough to answer. "I'll be fifty next month."

"Ha. I see." He paused again and his eyes lit up. He was on the right track to helping her out. "That's a very difficult time for a woman."

Betsy frowned, still puzzled, but remained quiet.

"Do you think that perhaps you are going through the change and that's why you feel the way you do?"

Betsy finally understood. Her husband was having an affair all because she is older. Not so long ago, she may have gone along with this: after all, she had been taught that women are only there to breed, serve and tempt men, so anything wrong had to be her fault. This time was different. She wasn't having it.

Her face turned a dark shade of red. She couldn't decide if it was from shame, humiliation or anger. She softly muttered, as to herself, "no, I… no that's… no…" She couldn't form a sentence, even in her head.

The priest took this as an encouragement to continue. "Have you been nice to Carl, like special meals, a clean house, things like that will usually keep a husband at home.." then he hesitated… "once, you know, once the attraction has faded?"

Betsy was astounded. Twenty years she had attended services in his church. Twenty years she had kneeled, stood, sat and taken communion from that man. Twenty years of believing that the church was all encompassing of what is just, fair, charitable and loving.

Her shoulders felt heavy with the sudden realization that maybe this was all a lie. Maybe this man was just there so others of his kind could cheat on their wives, or abandon their children without impunity. After all, everything he knew about women was from his mother, a spinster housekeeper and the twisted forms of femininity represented on television. Twenty years. A wave of pain twisted her chests and tears swelled up behind her eyes.

She rose almost knocking the chair down. "I'm sorry" she muttered. "I'm sorry. Everything is OK. I have to go," and ran out of the rectory.

Father Nelson made a blessing gesture as she left, allowing her to let herself out, saving her from any further social conversation; he then rubbed his hands, satisfied that he had probably saved another marriage. "Why, he puzzled, are women were so quick to blame men for all their hormonal surges." He shook his head and started shuffling some papers on his desk while calling out to his housekeeper for coffee.

Betsy rushed to her car and collapsed over the steering wheel, tears pouring out, unable to control the flow. She looked up at the old rectory and the thought of the priest perhaps spying on her produced a physical urge to leave. The expressway. Running away. No place to go. These thoughts ran through her head. She almost drove through a red light, nearly running over a terrified pedestrian. The elderly man glared at her from the curb.

Still shaking, she finally pulled into the mall parking and, out of habit, slipped the car in a space near the rear of the anchor store where few people ever parked.

Depression or anger, she couldn't define which she felt, but now an uncontrollable fear was surfacing, making all other feelings underneath seem insignificant. For a brief moment, she thought she was overreacting and all this would pass and things would be normal again. The moment went quickly.

She couldn't stay in the car; the security officer in a patrol jeep was already driving in her direction. The mall was anonymous enough, a walk might help.

The shops were almost empty on this Wednesday afternoon. Students were cramming for exams which would start in April, and most people were working somewhere else in town. The occasional housewife with toddlers in tow crossed her path and smiled at her. All Betsy could think of was: "This was me, a hundred years ago." She wished she could warn these younger women of what was in store for them once their womb, youthful energy and looks had been used up. She wondered how old Carl's girlfriend was.

A few older folks were 'mall walking' for their health and nodded to her as if she was one of them. Was she? Was this all that was left? She visualized herself throwing a large rock into one of those display windows. It would feel good, just to watch the glass shattering in a million pieces just as her life was.

This thought alone caused her pain. She sat on a bench, staring at nothing and ignoring the occasional shoppers who wondered … no, they didn't. No one cared who she was or why she was here. America, land of individuals. The 'me' land. No one cared. To many, she was just another housewife who was lucky she didn't have to work, or worse still, lazy and using her husband as a meal ticket.

Her breathing was almost back to normal. Regaining some composure, Betsy looked at the time and realized she should go home to prepare dinner and, with a quick shrug, was on the verge of dismissing her feelings as silly and childish. Then, she thought about father Nelson's advice and started laughing. No, no dinner tonight. Carl would probably not show anyway.

She stood up and jumped back in the present. That's when she noticed the travel agency in the wing by the food court. She suddenly knew what to do.

"May I help you" a woman, who seemed far too young to have a job, asked her.

"I'm not sure," Betsy said. I'd like to go to New York to see my daughter, but I don't have very much money.

"Well," the young woman answered thumbing through some papers, if you leave before Easter, it isn't too expensive. Are you thinking of going by bus or flying because if you fly, you'll have to drive to O'Hare."

"I want to fly. Don't you have busses that shuttle back and forth to the airport?" Betsy asked. She knew she had seen them around town before.

"Yeah, but that's extra. When do you want to go?"

"Now. Is that possible?"

"Everything is possible" the agent replied, "but… well, let me see what kind of last minute deal I can get for you. Do you have any other errands to run in the mall? I'll have the information for you in about 20 minutes."

Betsy wanted to know now, but realistically agreed to come back later.

Walking along the trendy shops she spotted a display offering crystals of every color and shape. Susan would like that. She impulsively walked in and studied all the different shapes before settling on a simple crystal ball, bubbles frozen in time within its orb, and a stand with brass snakes crawling toward and encircling the base of the ball.

"Maybe I can tell my future in that ball." She told the clerk, who glanced up but didn't respond.

Back at the travel store, the woman was busy with another customer, but motioned her to sit. "I'll be with you in a second."

Betsy looked up at the travel brochures lining the walls: Hawaii, Europe, the Bahamas... Places where she had never been. Places where she would never go. Although she never envied people who traveled, she now wondered how much she has missed out on. Everyday of her adult life had been a thrifty one. She was the one who paid the bills and had managed to build up a little nest egg, only a few hundred dollars, but enough to take her away for a while. Carl didn't know about this money but Betsy didn't think he'd care.

No one can afford real vacations with three kids and on a hardware clerk's salary, manager or not; plus, Carl had always refused to let her work. Not that she could do much of anything.

She had gone to college, but that was 30 years ago and the only job she ever had was as a sales clerk in a dress shop on Main Street, waiting for Carl to propose. Married at twenty five, twenty five years of marriage. Only superficial friends from church, none intimate, to speak of. Was it all a waste?

She wanted to say a silent prayer, but it only served to remind her of Father Nelson. She cringed at the notion and concentrated on the travel pictures on the far wall.

"I have the information you want," Betsy jumped out of her torpor, smiled at the agent, and changed seat for the one in front of the young woman's desk.

"You couldn't leave, like, right away," the agent continued, "but I did find a last minute ticket deal for you next Monday. The only thing I need to know is when you want to come back. To get the best price it has to be a weekday."

Betsy had not given a thought to ever coming back. Any date would do. Then she remembered that Mary Beth would be finishing school soon and she couldn't leave her here on her own for long, not with her dad the way he was acting up.

"Maybe the week after Easter, whichever day is best to get the cheapest ticket."

She also thought she should probably be close to home for her birthday, in case Carl really lived up to his promise.

The agent told her how much the fare was. It sounded reasonable to Betsy, although she had nothing to compare it to. She wasn't going to admit this to the woman, so she nodded and accepts the terms.

Fifteen minutes later, Betsy was at the bank getting the money, then back to the agency picking up the tickets, one for the flights, the other for the shuttle bus. Monday. That's it. Monday. Her heart was pounding with excitement mixed with fear.

The weekend went far better than Betsy expected. Carl, both Jr. and Sr. were working and neither one showed up for any of the dinners she had carefully prepared, not wanting them to suspect her plans. Mary Beth was cloistered in her room studying and Betsy occasionally brought her food or drinks. She thought of confiding in her, but, given her daughter's level of concentration and the pressure she was under, she changed her mind.

Monday morning, she waited until everyone was down for breakfast to tell them of her trip.

"Susan called last night," she lied, "and said she may need me for something, so I'm going." "Can't it wait for a bit? Mary Beth cried "I could go with you."

Betsy smiled "Maybe next time. You have your exams to worry about now." She picked up her bag and left without a glance back. "Wait up Mom," her unusually chivalrous son called up "I'll drive you to the bus".

He dropped her off at the bus depot without so much as a question or a goodbye hug. She watched him leave and found her ride.

##

The airport shuttle bus was almost empty on this rainy Monday morning, so Betsy sat in a window seat, then spread her bags out on the aisle seat to be sure no one would join her. She wasn't in a chatty mood.

The trip to O'Hare was uneventful, but, as much as she had picked up visitors there before, she was awed by the size of the terminal and the confusing areas of its inner workings. Take a deep breath and focus on one thing at the time, she told herself. First find the Airline counter, then security, then the gate.

With this information compartmentalized in her mind, she set out on her journey. She suddenly became conscious that this was her first flight ever, or, for that matter, her first time going anywhere by herself. A jolt of panic shocked her brain. What was she doing here?

Fear stopped her legs from moving and she had to lean against the security bar for a minute. She could turn back and go home. Visions of Carl mixed with Father Nelson and the life at home caused the fear to subside. She took a deep breath to dissipate the remaining doubts and continued on to the gate

It was three o'clock when the plane landed in Newark. Betsy knew there was no one waiting for her, because she hadn't told Susan about this trip. A surprise. She started having second thoughts. Maybe her daughter had moved since her last letter. Maybe she was living with a man, she shuddered at the thought. "Well," she thought, "too late. I'm here so, here we go."

She had gone to the library and mapped her way over the weekend, so the moves were encrypted in her head and she knew all she had to do was find the Path train and get off, well, she would remember when she saw it.

Betsy found the right stop, walked up to the street and gave Susan's address to a nice-looking, seemingly friendly taxi driver.

She saw an expanse of brownish grass in front of a building where the cab finally slowed down, but he continued, turned left and stopped in front of a gloomy looking apartment building, the likes of it Betsy had never seen before, having avoided any urban contact all her life. She paid the man, wondering if you tipped taxi drivers and how much was fair. She left him the small change from the fare. It suddenly dawned on her that she knew nothing about life outside of her small town, apart from what she had seen on television.

Betsy tentatively opened the door to the building and rang the bell for apartment 506. No answer. It was now almost five o'clock. If her daughter was not home, she may be out working all night.

She took a deep breath in an attempt to fight the panic that was, once again, rising in her chest. She rang again.

This time a voice came on the intercom. "Who's this" a young high pitched voice inquired.

Betsy didn't recognize her daughter's voice and was starting to sweat. "I'm looking for Susan? Is this the right apartment?"

"Oh yeah, the voice said," Betsy let out a sigh of relief.

"But, the voice continued, she's not here right now. Anything I can tell her for you?" "This is her mom" Betsy informed her. "Can I come in?" "Oh, did she expect you? She never told me about your coming over."

"It's sort of a surprise. Can I come in?"

Betsy could tell the young woman was hesitating. After all this was New York and she knew people just didn't let people in their homes just like that.

Betsy insisted, "Why don't you let me in and I can show you my ID through the peephole before you open the door." "That sounds fair." The woman replied.

A buzzing sounded and the locking mechanism clicked on. Betsy had seen this in movies, so she tentatively pulled the door and, sure enough it opened.

The apartment was small; you walked right into the kitchen from the corridor. The living room, across from a counter which served as table and work area, was furnished with eclectic pieces from various eras and of dubious quality. There were no curtains in the living room windows, or in either of the closet-sized bedrooms that opened up to the main room.

Melissa was a petite woman with red hair and freckles who introduced herself as Susan's room mate. After exchanging pleasantries, they both snacked on pizza until her daughter finally came home sometime after 10.

"Mom! What are you doing here?" Susan exclaimed, not sure of the appropriate feelings she should be displaying.

"I don't know yet," Betsy replied with the uneasy feeling that she'd be in the way of her daughter's life.

After the initial shock, Susan hugged her mom and they both sank into the brown sofa whose previous owners had carved craters in three different areas.

After the usual "You can sleep in my room, I'll sleep here" and "no, I wouldn't hear of it" and "sorry I barged in" and "sorry I wish I'd known you were coming"… they just sat and stared at each other for a while.

Betsy went through her bag and found the crystal ball purchased at the mall. She wordlessly handed it to Susan. Her daughter laughed and said this was perfect, considering she was thinking of getting a second job as a fortune teller. Seeing her mom, eyes down, staring at her hands, she knew there was something seriously wrong.

"OK, mom, I know you. What's going on? And, what on earth would you have done if Melissa hadn't been here?"

Betsy stared at her fingers, embarrassed, "I don't know. I never thought about that when I decided to come. I just…" she started.

"Mom, what's wrong? You'll have to tell me sooner or later, so why don't you just say it. You didn't come all the way here to say Hi."

She paused. "It's always been a problem between us. We know when there is something wrong with the other, but we never talk about it. I've changed, mom, I'm all grown up now and you'll have to trust me." She cocked her head, and smiled at her mom. "Please?"

Betsy looked up at her daughter as if seeing her for the first time. She was a grown woman. "A grown woman who hasn't made any of my mistakes yet." She mused. "Maybe she's the 'me' I could have been."

Susan's long brown hair was tied in a fashionably messy pony tail, her big brown eyes, her ordinary, but slim and attractive figure looked familiar. "Yes that could have been me twenty five years ago." A surge of affection rose in her chest.

"Well, she hesitated, your dad has not been around much lately and..." she stopped, bit her lips, tears starting to swell up in her eyes.

Melissa quietly walked out and soon Betsy could hear the television in the other room. "I don't know Susan. It's me I guess, look at me, I'm a fifty year old frump from middle of nowhere Illinois. There's nothing left for anyone to like here."

Susan knew better than to contradict her mom. She just put her arm behind Betsy and allowed her mother's head to rest on her shoulder and thought how many times she had wished her mom had done that for her. "What am I going to do, Susan? My life is over. I have no job; you kids have you own lives. What am I going to do?"

They sat silently, Betsy sobbing softly, for what seemed like hours. She finally calmed down. Susan took charge. She could see the exhaustion in her mom's face and understood that nothing more would be said tonight. "Why don't we just sleep on it? Tomorrow, I have a lunch shift, so I can take you with me and you can roam around the village while I work. I'm sure you'll feel much better by tomorrow night."

Betsy slept surprisingly well on the lumpy makeshift bed and was awakened by Melissa's soft singing voice coming in from the adjacent kitchen.

"Good morning". Melissa turned.

"Oh, I'm sorry; I didn't mean to wake you up. It's such a bad habit I have of always humming or singing."

Betsy smiled. "It isn't a bad habit. You have a lovely voice." This caused Melissa to chuckle. "Thanks, I wish the casting people felt the same way."

"You're an actress?" asked Betsy, wondering how the subject had not come up the previous evening.

"If only people who make a living from acting can be called that, I'd have to say no. I work as a waitress like Susan but I'm one of the thousands trying to break into the Broadway scene."

"How interesting." That's all Betsy could respond. She had never known anyone like her before. A real actress! She decided she might just like New York.

Susan wasn't so perky in the morning. She dragged herself through the living room, grabbed a cup of coffee and disappeared into the bathroom. Betsy smiled thinking how people never change much.

Getting Susan up and ready for school had always been a tedious and constant work of love, deceits and briberies since her first day of kindergarten.

She waited until her daughter was out and quickly showered and dressed herself. Susan was ready. There was no mention of breakfast as they left, walked west then north on Broadway.

The west Village was crammed with traffic, horns blaring, and people rushing back and forth seemingly bound for somewhere specific. Susan pointed to the more interesting shops or famous buildings, but Betsy was just absorbing the essence of the place. Details would come later. In her entire life, she had never seen this many people at one time.

The two women finally stopped in front of "Le Grand Lapin", the restaurant where Susan worked. After sitting down for coffee and oven fresh croissants the chef insisted on giving them, Susan drew a small map of the area and wrote the restaurant's phone number with specific instructions to call for any reason whatsoever. They would meet later under the arch in Washington Square.

The city was warm today and Betsy was glad that she had brought a lighter jacket. There were buds dangling from the trees, some of which had started to open up. Betsy, with her polyester black pants, white shirt tucked in the elastic waist band, and a gray polyester jacket bought at Kmart last year, felt frumpy, walking among the beautiful and trendy Village denizens. Her own mousy colored, home-permed brown hair, gray roots showing, was also no match for the array of colors and shapes women carried on their heads. She looked more like the furtive, pathetic-looking characters she saw hanging around the less frequented alleyways.

Soon enough, though, she found herself completely enthralled by everything around her. She had never known this kind of excitement, mixed with a bit of fear that completely overwhelms the senses. Now she understood the attraction people had to this city. It was energizing. It made her feel young again. It made her smile. She walked for hours, her feet just floating over the warm pavement.

She met Susan in the square and they walked home, one tired from a hard day at work, the other dizzy from too much stimulation. Melissa was working the dinner shift, so they sat in the apartment alone, facing each other, at the minuscule café table near the window.

"I'm sorry, Susan, about yesterday." Betsy said when she and her daughter finally sat to a dinner of frozen lasagna and bread sticks all warmed in the microwave. "I feel much better today. This is a great place and I'm glad you look so happy." Susan looked at her surroundings. "Mom, I don't know if you noticed, but this apartment is smaller than the living room at home. I can touch the couch from the kitchen. Great isn't the word I would use for it." Betsy smiled. "It's fine. Besides, I also meant the city, your work, Melissa. It all seems like so much life."

"You have a great life too, mom". Betsy's smile faded.

"Today, I saw women my age, probably older and they looked beautiful. They looked like they have a purpose in life, a place to go. I'd like to have that too."

"But you do have a place to go. A nice home. What are you telling me mom?"

Betsy hesitated. "I think your dad, well, I think he's having an affair." She hoped Susan would jump up and decry this statement and tell her this was impossible, but she didn't. She just looked and stared, waiting for more.

"He's been late almost every night for the last while. I went to the store on a weekend when he was supposed to be working and he wasn't there. He doesn't even bother to make believable excuses anymore. Your brother can't look me in the eyes either. He knows."

"What are you going to do?" was all Susan can say, trying to look surprised. Everyone but Betsy had always known about Carl's roving eyes, but it was part of a status quo no one wanted to disrupt. Betsy looked at her daughter trying to read her thoughts, but could not bring herself to admit that perhaps she had been the only one to be fooled all these years.

"I don't know. I have no job, no purpose, no place to go. I don't know. Even if I left him, how would I live?"

Susan didn't respond but just came to her mom and gave her a hug. "You can stay here as long as you want." She said in her most comforting tone. So many questions came to her: what about her brother and sister? What about everything she had grown up believing in? But, she knew enough to let her mom tell her in her own time.

"Tomorrow, she continued, we're going up town. It's my day off and I'll show you Broadway and all those places where the morning news shows compete for a crowd to cheer them on. Is that OK?" Betsy smiled.

Nothing more could be said for now and she was grateful to her daughter for the respite. "Sounds great. I can't wait. And Susan, thanks for letting me stay here." Then she hesitated and said something which never came easy for her "I love you Susan." They sat together for a while, silent, both wondering what would happen next.

##

Betsy woke up the next day and heard Melissa and Susan whispering in the other room, or maybe on the phone; she couldn't be sure. She was surprised her daughter was already up and glanced at the wall clock. It was past nine: she had not slept that late in years. They'd already missed the morning shows. There was time, she could do it another day.

Not wanting to intrude on the girls' conversation, she slipped into the bathroom. That space reminded her of a jigsaw puzzle she had once put together: a white toilet, a stand-alone sink with various cleaning and sanitary supplies crowded under it and a medicine cabinet filled with over the counter pharmaceuticals and make-up, the whole thing protected by a mirror door barely large enough to reflect her head.

The bathtub was stained from years of use and the shower head impaired by whatever minerals were part of the New York City water system. And again, no curtains hung in the window. Betsy took a quick shower, considerate of the fact that this was the only facility in the apartment.

She came out of the bathroom wrapped in a towel, hair in curly Q's glued to her forehead and drawing circles around her ears with the occasional gray strands sticking out like steel wires. Susan was just walking out of her room.

"Oh Mom, I didn't know you were up" she said too quickly, shocked by the years that had crept up on her mother's face, only in the last year.

She couldn't remember the transition period. It was as if time had played a cruel joke and triggered her mother to age overnight. "We'll have breakfast, and leave after." She continued. "There is a lot I want to show you around the city and, if it's ok with you, we'll meet Melissa for lunch and you can see Broadway!"

"That sounds marvelous. You know what? Maybe I'll treat us all to a Broadway play." Betsy said with enthusiasm, on her way to the bedroom to get dressed. "How much are tickets these days?" She did have at least an extra $100. to spend.

"Most are over a hundred dollars each." Susan said casually.

Betsy felt a bubble burst in her stomach. Wasn't there anything at all she could do for anyone? Tears swelled in her eyes and she hurried to her daughter's bedroom to dress before anyone could see them. "Hey, Melissa cried from the kitchen, maybe we can get 'twofers' cheap or there might be standing room tickets for some plays."

Betsy knew even at half price, she could never treat the girls to the theater and, just looking at the menu where Susan worked, treating them to a special meal was also out of the question.

She sat on the bed, shoulders hunched, eyes staring at the fat that lined her midriff, now protruding out of the towel. She stood up and dressed slowly, deliberately delaying having to face the girls again. For the first time in her life, she felt not only dependant and sad, but also poor. She remembered some of the homeless women she had seen on television and suddenly knew there was not much separating her from that fate. She put on a drab shapeless dress, one with flowers dimmed by many machine wash and reminding of some worn out upholstery.

Betsy walked back into the living room where Susan and Melissa were gulping down cereals with soy milk; she joined them, careful not to complain about the unusual taste of this breakfast. After all, she was the poor relative and had no place demanding anything from her daughter.

##

The two women had been walking for almost two hours. "Wow" was all Betsy could finally say, overwhelmed by the sights, sounds and energy of the city and amazed at the fact that she could walk this much and still feel energized. She had not said a word since leaving the apartment.

The veil of sadness had slowly lifted as the blood flowed to her briskly moving body. They had walked up to mid-town and, with Susan as a tour guide, Betsy now knew some of the most important historical and demographic facts of each neighborhood they crossed.

The sun was getting warm and there was a summer feel to the air. Both women were hungry and ready to settle down for lunch.

Melissa was on time and the three chose an inexpensive deli that offered sandwiches so filled with meats and dressings that one was more than enough to satisfy both mother and daughter's appetite. Melissa had a small salad.

"Is everything set?" Susan asked her friend. "Yes, we just have to go backstage at the theater.

They'll be there at two." Susan asked if there had been problems, and her friend shook her head. "They all have mothers somewhere, so they were very good about it. Besides, I've helped them with catering before. They owe me." she said.

Betsy didn't understand what was going on and tried to pretend she was watching people strolling passed the restaurant. She felt uncomfortable, an intruder in their lives, now wishing she hadn't come.

"We've arranged for you to see the backstage of a Broadway show." Susan said. "I don't want to be any trouble." That was all Betsy could say, crawling back up to the high end of her roller coaster. Broadway. She was shaking at the thought of perhaps meeting some important star.

They walked past other theaters that had stars' names on billboards, many of whom Betsy recognized from having seen them interviewed on the morning show she faithfully watched every day. Her heart was pounding when the three women finally slipped into an alley, stopped at a door, a hole in the wall, really, and Melissa knocked.

A young man opened the door and welcomed the threesome with hugs and pecks on the cheeks. Betsy felt a little uneasy but they were not bear hugs, just dainty squeezes, so she decided it was okay.

They made the introductions and were joined by two other young men who stood, staring at her while Susan and Melissa exchanged news with them. This made Betsy feel even more awkward.

Finally Susan faced her mom, put her hands on her shoulder and declared: "OK mom, this is it. These guys here are make-up artists and hair stylists. They're going to give you a make-over."

Betsy had seen hundreds of those on Oprah, but she never thought of herself as make-over material.

"But Susan, I don't think that's a good idea. What would your father say?"

She read the look in her daughter's eyes and lowered her head. "Of course, why should I care about Carl," she thought. "I guess that's ok." She timidly looked at the 'artists', wondering what would come next but afraid to ask.

She had home-trimmed, colored and permed her own hair for years and wondered what they could possibly do to make her look better. She anticipated the disappointment that was inevitable, but kept quiet.

Susan had her slip into a white shapeless dress and they started working around her. Jon, one of the stylists, kept turning her head this way and that with a studious look on his face. Her hair was washed, cut, separated by what looked like aluminum foil, and, then Rick, the other man started staring at her face.

She closed her eyes, pretending this was a dream and she would wake up back to her Cinderella self in the morning. The hands on her face were somehow comforting and she just gave in to the moment. She drifted off fighting tears of regret, thinking how she had never been touched so gently.

"Mom!" Betsy was startled out of her semi hypnotic state and opened her eyes. There was a new woman in the room, staring at her. It took her a minute to realize she was staring at her own image: the hair was an ashy brown with dark blond highlights and the curls were gone. A few strands for a fringe and simple, but striking layers emphasized her now oversized eyes.

Her eyebrows were all but gone and her first thought was that she looked surprised, but her thin lips were now fuller and her cheeks somehow more youthful. "Wow" was, once again, all she could say. "Do you like it Mom?" She just kept staring. "It's amazing. That doesn't look like me. I'm not sure I can show myself like this."

They were all smiling, quite satisfied with their work. "Now I know where you get your looks, Susan" one of the young men said. Melissa, who had been missing from the group, walked in with an arm full of clothes. "I have to go back to work. I'm working the dinner shift again, but I dug those out of wardrobe. They'll never miss anything. There must be a gazillion dresses in there." She dumped her load on a chair, hugged everyone goodbye and left.

An hour later, Susan and Betsy were sharing a happy hour drink at a fashionable, but reasonably priced restaurant near the theatre. Betsy had chosen a suit, a linen skirt and jacket, navy blue with white trim and had been convinced to take a simple black linen dress as well. She insisted that she would pay the owner for the clothes as soon as she returned home. She felt like a new person.

Betsy was watching the crowd, a sophisticated group of men and women, eating and talking about plays they had seen or were about to see. She now looked like she belonged, but knew this was all an illusion. Both mother and daughter took advantage of the hors d'oeuvres served at happy hour to pretend they were having dinner out. They left just before curtain call and walked home again.

Over the next few days, Betsy fell into the younger women's routine, helping with meals and keeping the apartment clean for them. Only Mary Beth had called to find out how she was; when Betsy asked about her dad, her normally talkative daughter evaded the question and made some excuse to hang up.

She had found local shops and learned that if you played your cards right, you could get better deals on meats and vegetables. Betsy was surprised that all this came so easy to her, a sheltered housewife from the Midwest who had never had to interact with food providers except for the cashier at the supermarket.

Sunday came and Betsy knew she had to go to church. "You just don't throw away that many years of your life in one sweep," she thought. Susan suggested a local parish, attended mostly by the Hispanic community, but one that would be friendly and not too intimidating. She herself had only been twice to attend a friend's wedding and the christening of a neighbor's child, but she volunteered to accompany her mother.

The sky was overcast so they both carried umbrellas in their tote bags. Betsy and Susan entered through the massive metal doors and settled in one of the last pews near the back.

The church was small, ornate on the outside with cornices and statues, but dark and solemn inside. A statue of the Sacred Heart was in a prominent corner with red luminaries and a Virgin Mary opened her arms in the opposite corner, blue cape, eyes cast down seemingly staring at the votive candles, most of them lit up in their blue glass holders.

A procession entered the church led by a gentle-looking young man, dressed up with the appropriate garbs; altar boys surrounded him, some carrying vessels with burning incense, others holding the holy books for the upcoming ceremony.

The priest was young and had a soft, calming quality about him. Betsy felt an immediate attraction to this man of God, mentally comparing him to his mid-western counterpart. She cringed at the thought of Father Nelson and his callous ways and immediately felt guilty for the anger still burning in her heart. She asked God for forgiveness and help in finding her way. How she had changed in such a short time.

She tried to follow the rituals of the mass, but her mind strayed to her experiences of the last week. A new world had opened up and she didn't want to let go of it. She knew she couldn't stay with Susan forever, but she had crossed the depression bridge and was now visualizing a new life for herself. Maybe she could make it, after all. There might be life beyond Carl.

The sermon sounded like a poem, one she couldn't understand, but every word soothing both to her body and her soul. She just let the Spanish rhythm of it lull her into a state of joy and peace. Communion and final blessing came too soon. Betsy couldn't or maybe didn't want to leave this sanctuary.

Susan finally pulled her arm and they both left the pew, the last ones to leave the church. The sun had broken through the clouds and a wrap of sunshine found its way on Betsy's shoulders. Father Pascal was still on the steps talking to parishioners. Betsy had to meet this man. She just stood near the assembly and waited her turn. Sensing her stare, the priest took a leave from the group and came towards her.

"Good morning Mrs.???" "I'm Betsy" she quickly said.

She almost blurted her maiden name, but held back, surprised, but unable to admit her marriage to Carl to this man of God.

"I'm from the Midwest but right now I'm staying with my daughter, she continued, pointing in the general direction where Susan stood.

"Welcome to our parish. I hope you enjoyed the service. Do you understand Spanish?"

"Not very well, Betsy confessed, I learned a bit in high school, but that was years ago."

She wanted to go on and tell this man her story. She wanted to find a home in the fold of this community: it was poor, but somehow that is what she liked about it. She too was poor. She could fit-in here.

They exchanged more banalities, Betsy promised to be back for Palm Sunday the following week, and left with Susan, feeling glad but also a little disturbed. She knew she must see that man again.

Both women went home, changed into more casual clothes, packed a picnic, a blanket and a book, and rode the subway to Central Park. Lying on the blanket after lunch, eyes resting on the skyline looking south, Betsy sensed a kinship to this city as if it recognized her and wanted her to stay. She let herself daydream and actually fell asleep next to her daughter who was totally immersed in a mystery novel.

##

Over the following week, Betsy became even more rooted into her daughter's daily routine, but this time, it included rising bright and early and going to mass before the girls were even up. She had always been a devout Catholic, but she had never experienced religion as it was practiced here. She was getting a lot of satisfaction just listening to the melodic Spanish words and bought a book to teach herself the basics of this language at a local used book store.

On Friday, father Pascal caught her before she had a chance to escape. "Betsy, hello. I noticed you here every day this week. I'm glad you're enjoying our services."

"I do, very much," Betsy answered. "I", she hesitated, "I need to find some peace and your church seems to make everything seem easier."

She lowered her eyes, unable to confide in this relative stranger yet. She just wanted to keep healing and deal with her problems later when they didn't hurt so much. Avoidance is sometimes the only way to heal a wound.

"I understand", the priest continued, "there are times in everyone's life when everything gets confused. I'm just glad that our humble parish suits your mood. If you ever want to talk, you know you are welcome to visit our house and have tea with the family."

Betsy didn't understand. Of course priests don't have families and this one looked young, but not that much so that he still lived at home. Father Pascal noticed her puzzled look and burst out laughing.

"I'm sorry. I should have told you. No, I'm not married and my parents are still living on a farm in Florida. I live at the Casa de Maria. It's sort of a refuge where women, children and sometimes whole families come to if they find themselves homeless or needing some help and support. They are my family, so I warn you, if you come, don't expect a quiet sanctuary with a big fancy desk. Our house is furnished by what our parishioners give us and when it needs repairs, it's also done by the charity of a friend or one of the residents. In our home, it's all for one and one for all."

"It sounds interesting." Betsy emphatically responded, thinking she had to visit that place where real life happened and where people's problems were likely much more important than her own. "I better go. Susan will wonder where I am."

"I look forward to seeing you on Palm Sunday. We do a procession around the block and I'm sure you'll enjoy the choir: they really outdo themselves for that special feast."

She waved and walked back, smiling, feeling, for some reason, like she had a purpose in life.

She later joined the morning show crowd near Time Square, dressed in her new suit, pretending to belong. She was finally gaining some perspective on her life back home. The pain was receding and she was now sure she may have over-reacted. She vowed to fix everything as soon as she returned home.

The girls both worked that Saturday, so Betsy decided to take the subway to Coney Island and see the ocean close-up for the first time. It was hard to decide whether the various scents were pleasant or nauseating, but life was teeming. Children, glad to be free of winter clothing were running on the boardwalk, or throwing sand at each other, some daring to wade in the still cold salty water.

Betsy was wearing a bright blue cotton pair of pants bought at a thrift shop near Susan's apartment. Rummaging through the bric-a-brac on the boardwalk, she found matching straw hat and bag which she spent almost her last pennies on. She'd have to borrow from Susan or call home for more money.

That thought brought her mood down for a while, but the sun and surf soon had her smiling again. People argued, laughed, walked hand in hand, all so alive and real. She went home early, saw a note that the girls had gone on dates and settled on the couch with a book borrowed from Melissa, a mystery with some woman detective who seem to have it all, in spite of being single and living in a renovated garage. She envied her.

The Palm Sunday service was something she had never seen before. The joy and exaltation of the crowd could not be compared with the somber services that had been part of her life so far.

Religion had always been something serious which emphasized sacrifice over self-indulgent events like fiestas. She suddenly realized how in just two weeks, she had learn so much about human nature. Television, she concluded, did not do justice to real life.

She was reminded of the travel brochure in the agent's office back home and all the places where she would never go and for the first time she felt some regrets. She shrugged it off, thinking about the children and happy times they had had over the years.

When she got home, she prepared another picnic and the three women took the subway to Central Park, this time carrying a scrabble game board and some playing cards. Betsy had finally found a place in her soul where she could be at peace and was finally learning to enjoy the feeling.

That week went by quickly, with Thursday and Good Friday filled with religious rituals and prayers. Betsy attended all the ceremonies and saw another side to the community.

Many members were crying when reminded of the passion of Christ, no doubt thinking about their own suffering and pain.

After the three o'clock service, father Pascal ran out to catch up with her on the church steps. Hi Betsy, wait up!" She stopped and turned to face the priest.

"Are you planning on staying in New York for a while?" he asked. "Well," Betsy said, "I have to fly back next week, but," she hesitated, "but I'd like to stay longer. In fact I have never felt so happy and wish I could stay here for good."

"What about your family back home?" the priest asked.

"Well, my children are all grown. They really don't need me anymore and my husband..."

"Your husband?" the priest asked prompting her to continue.

He had believed she was a widow or, at least living alone.

"Well, he's, like, he's" She looked up apprehensively. "He's been sort of been running around on me." They were both silent for a minute.

"Are you sure?" The priest inquired, not wanting to judge before knowing all the facts.

"Yes, I'm pretty sure." Betsy answered reluctantly. "I think even Susan here in New York knew before I did. That's why I'm here; I didn't know what to do. He hasn't even called me since I've been here." She confessed blushing from the embarrassment.

She was so ashamed. Tears were now rolling down her cheeks, she recaptured the despair she had felt at home and braced herself for father Pascal to tell her she had only herself to blame her for her problems. He didn't.

"How can a man not appreciate such a wonderful woman as you?" Betsy raised her eyes to the priest, surprised by his reaction.

"If you want to talk about it with me or even with one of the women in the 'family', please come over any time." He paused. "Actually, I was asking you how long you would be here because one of the women who helps out with managing the house has to go and take care of her own mother back on the west coast, and I thought you may be interested in joining us."

He smiled apologetically, "It doesn't pay much, but it includes room and board. I kind of figured you may feel like your daughter may need her space back."

She looked at him, surprised and speechless. "Well, let's put that aside for now. Regina isn't leaving until June, so there is still over a month to go. But, think about it, that is, if you choose to come back to us. Most of our residents speak Spanish, but I've seen you carrying a Spanish lesson book so you could probably pick up on the conversations in no time. Just seeing you everyday in church tells me you're the kind of person we would welcome to our family."

More tears started streaming down Betsy's face. "You really think I could do that? A job. A real job?" Father Pascal smiled. "You've been doing a 'real job' for many years, Betsy. You'd just be trading one family for another. Think about it."

He smiled, patted her on the shoulder and walked away to talk to another parishioner. Betsy stood for a while on the sidewalk, stunned, but her feet finally carried her back to her daughter's apartment.

She didn't tell Susan about the encounter thinking she should let it sink-in first. Then both girls worked lunch on Saturday and had dates that night so the occasion never arose to discuss the offer.

On Sunday, she was awed by all the frills and adornments which accompanied the resurrection of Christ at the Church. She even talked to someone and understood most of the woman's reply.

After the service, she could only wave to father Pascal who, flanked by the entire congregation which had organized an Easter Lunch, waved back and motioned her to call him.

She got home at eleven and called Mary Beth. She found her alone, but ready to go to the late Easter service at church, the only one she attended, save for Christmas, and then have brunch with a friend from college. Mary Beth didn't know where her father and brother were and Betsy was glad for her daughter's independence and happy nature.

Susan and Melissa were still asleep, off work for the day, exhausted from the previous late night-out. Both had worked dinner shifts that week and deserved to sleep late. Betsy decided to make a special lunch of salad, soup, omelet and home made biscuits.

Going home didn't seem so bad anymore. She was feeling stronger and almost, just almost, ready to face Carl. She thought 'confront' but mentally shook her head and decided that she could now just face him and deal with whatever he would tell her in a rational way.

Susan crawled out of bed around noon and noticed her mom humming a song under her breath while cooking. She frowned, wondering what the occasion was, then smiled, remembering happier times when her mom always hummed while cooking. "Boy, this smells good! What's happening mom? Did you go to church yet?"

Betsy turned to look at her daughter and wished she was the kind of mother who could hug her kids at will. "Happy Easter, sweetheart. Yes, I just got back." She hesitated, turned back to the stove, but then decided the time was right. She turned to face her daughter. "You won't believe what happened." She took a deep breath. "Father Pascal offered me a job on Friday."

Surprised, Susan first wondered if her mom had been drinking, but saw no evidence of this. Then she thought of what would happen is her mom stayed and felt a pang of fear. Having her for a few weeks was fine, but forever? She could never pay for an apartment of her own here. "Wow" was all she managed to say.

"Well, it's actually a job at La Casa, helping manage the place. Father Pascal says it's hard to find people who are interested in a job that demands a lot of dedication, offers no benefits and pays so little."

She sensed Susan's discomfort and quickly added: "I'd get room and board." She stopped and laughed. "Can you imagine me with a job?"

Susan relaxed. Well, it may not be so bad after all but they really had to sit and have a serious conversation. She knew her mom was leaving soon and they had never really discussed her situation yet. Maybe she is ready now, she thought.

"Mom, why don't you come and sit down? I know Melissa won't be up for a while, so we can talk."

Betsy stirred the soup, eyed her biscuits to make sure they were ready to bake and sat on the well worn couch, waiting for her daughter to start.

"What are you going to do, Mom" she simply asked.

"I don't know." Betsy answered. "But I want you to know that I could never have gone through this time without you. I think I'm ready to go home now."

"What will you tell dad? Will you come back?" Betsy lowered her head. Her chest was starting to tighten, anticipating an anxiety attack, but it relaxed on its own. "I don't know, probably not." she replied. "I'm sure your dad will have some explanation. I don't know. Maybe I over-reacted to this whole thing and I'll just go home and it'll feel right again. You know, when you're too close to something, you can't see the forest for the trees. I'm just glad you allowed me to stay here with you."

"Anytime, mom. And, please, come back if…" she hesitated, "things don't work out. I'm here for you."

Betsy finally gathered the courage to hug her daughter.

"Thank you. And Susan, you know I love you." "I love you too, mom." Susan said, "and I think I see a happy ending in this crystal ball." She smiled.

They stayed embraced for a while and then heard Melissa stirring in the other room. Betsy got up and resumed her chopping for the salad.

A sweet whiff of tomatoes and celery was now floating in the apartment mixed with the baking aroma and the three women eventually sat to enjoy the home made lunch. Melissa even produced a bottle of wine from her room and they just sat, chatted through the afternoon.

Betsy was now looking forward to going home. It felt right. She had made too much of things. She could handle whatever happened now. In fact, she looked forward to baking in her own kitchen and shopping at Pick & Save. She even wondered if she shouldn't get her perm back. Maybe her old life wasn't so bad. She even smiled, imagining Carl's look when he saw her new, improved, look.

That week went by quickly and Betsy never had a chance to talk to father Pascal, even after the early mass which she still attended everyday. God was good, she thought, everything will be fine. She believed it and wished it at the same time. She tried to say goodbye to the priest on her last day, but he was talking with a group of women and did not see Betsy leave.

Both Susan and Melissa rode the train to the airport with Betsy and she left, promising to return and asking them to visit. Susan slipped a few dollars in he mom's pocket: "take a cab when you get home, I don't want you to walk with your luggage and all."

Betsy tried to refuse, but eventually accepted, finally realizing that their roles were now reversed. She was the one being taken care of and wasn't sure how to handle it.

The flight was uneventful. Betsy hadn't talked to Carl since leaving, but knew from Mary Beth that he was mostly working and had not asked about her whereabouts. "Mind you," her daughter had said, "I'm not home much what with the exams and all." He had probably forgotten when she was coming back, but she'd find her way home from the bus.

She shivered when the bus stopped at the depot. It was cloudy and much colder than it had been in New York, but that wasn't it. She was scared. The new found strength was back in New York. She was cringing at having to face Carl. But there was no choice. "Everything will be fine" she kept trying to convince herself, fighting off anxiety.

I was after five when the taxi dropped her off at home. The car was in the driveway, so Carl was home.

She took a deep breath, put her bags down and found the key to the house. As quietly as she could, she let herself in: she didn't want him to surprise her first.

She would have the upper hand if she found him first. She walked in the kitchen and recognized the familiar smell of her own home cooking. Funny, she thought, how long someone's scent lingers in a house. A comforting wave washed over her and she smiled.

Carl wasn't on the first floor, but she thought she heard some noise upstairs. She picked up her bags and started up the stairs. Unpacking would give her a reason not to look at him directly.

She was out of breath when she reached the second floor landing, not from the climb or the weight of the luggage, but from the terror she felt in anticipation of her next move. She paused when she saw that the bedroom door was closed.

She took a deep breath and walked over to the door. That's when she thought she heard a woman's voice. "Was it Mary Beth looking for something in the bedroom, or, worse still," Betsy thought, "borrowing her bed to be with a boy?"

Her anger shifted to righteousness and she opened the door in one movement. Carl was lying in bed with a chemically red-headed woman nestled in the crook of his arm, both giggling over some private joke.

A scream escaped Betsy's heart and both bodies on the bed rose up and stared in stunned surprise.

Betsy just dropped her bags, walked out of the room and ran back downstairs. She walked out, leaving the front door open, and started walking aimlessly.

It was dark and a cold chill was whipping her face from the West. She couldn't remember how long it had been since she had stormed out of the house, but the bitter cold was driving her back to shelter. As she rounded the corner of her street, she saw that the car was gone and walked back to the house.

She was relieved, but paused just long enough to recapture her indignation and some of the anger. Mary Beth was at home, totally ignorant of what had happened. "Hey Mom! I thought you'd be home earlier! Sorry I didn't meet you at the station, I was studying for my last exam at the library and totally lost track of time."

Her bubbly nature always rubbed off on Betsy, but not tonight. Seeing her mother soberly staring at her, she realized something was wrong. "What's up mom? I'm sorry about forgetting." Then she looked around and saw that there was no suitcase or bag around. "Where are your bags? Did you leave them at the station?"

Betsy walked passed her daughter and just sat on the living room couch, still unable to talk. Mary Beth followed her, now concerned that something was seriously wrong. "Did something happen to Dad? Or Susan? Please mom, what's wrong?"

"I'm sorry," Betsy said. "No, no one died." Maybe me, she thought to herself. Mary Beth just sat next to her mom, waiting for her to continue. Betsy turned and looked at her daughter, glad to see that she had been spared the pain she now felt.

"I," she started, "I think I have to go again." "What do you mean, why?" Mary Beth asked.

Betsy shook her head, trying to clear the thoughts that were assaulting her consciousness. "It's your dad. I have to go."

She thought of Susan, Melissa, Father Pascal and his community and failed to understand what she thought she would find by coming back here. She now realized she had been in denial and nothing in this marriage was worth salvaging. She looked at her youngest daughter and tried to smile, but to Mary Beth, her broken smile looked more like a wince of pain.

Betsy thought she had to put herself together if only for her daughter' sake. "I'll be going back to New York as soon as I can. Someone there offered me a job and it sounds really good. I have to go. Do you understand Mary?"

Her daughter lowered her eyes. She had known about her father's antics, but never realized it had gone that far. "Are you sure, Mom?" Betsy put her hand on her daughter's shoulder. "I wasn't this morning, but I am now."

"What about me?" That was all Mary Beth could think about saying.

"Well, what about you? What do you want to do?"

"My exams are just about over. Can I go with you? I have good grades, I'm sure I could graduate next year at NYU or Columbia. If not, I could always take a year off to help you out. You can't leave me here. I saved money from my job; I can pay my own way!" She finally said with fear in her voice.

"I don't think I want to leave you here either," she smiled sadly "I'm the one with no money. If you can pay my way too, we have a deal."

Betsy tightened her grip on her daughter's shoulder and they fell in each other's arms, released by the tears they were now both shedding. "Mary, do you mind if I share your room tonight?" "Sure mom. Let's call Susan."

##

Father Pascal was fussing around a miniature flower garden in front of La Casa when Betsy called out to him. "Hi father," she said. "Is that job still open?"

He rose from his task, hands muddied from planting and digging, sweat pouring from his forehead. His smile warmed Betsy's heart. "If you can promise me to take over the upkeep of this garden, it is." He said wiping his hands on his overall to grab hers earnestly. "Welcome to La Casa De Maria. Oh, and Happy Birthday."

##

CLARA

"What on earth is this dress about?" Those were the first words Clara ever said to me. My first impression was that Clara was an arrogant, brash woman wearing a multi color, ill-fitting jacket, a woman who really should not discuss other people's dress choices.

It took a while for me to warm up to her and see Clara as she really was: a funny, delightful woman who only occasionally turned judgmental and often complained about how others always complained. She was originally from the islands but had just moved to New York from England where she had acquired the most delicate and, truth be told, one of the sexiest English accents I had ever heard. At a time before sexual harassment became fashionable, male callers felt compelled to comment about her voice and tried to find out more about this exotic-sounding lady.

We worked together for a couple of years and became friends, hanging-out in the city whenever we had a chance. I then went back to graduate school in Chicago, and Clara went to Miami where she had found a better job and hoped to finish nursing school, a dream of hers since coming to this country.

From then on, we connected by mail over the holidays and the occasional phone calls on our respective birthdays. By that time, it was more habitual practice than genuine friendship, so, twenty years later, when we coincidently both returned to work in Manhattan the same year, we threatened to get together, but it hadn't worked out.

A few months ago, I was walking from a luncheon date downtown and ran into her. As it were, we both had an hour to spare and reconnected at a coffee shop. Clara had aged well, much more gracefully than I had, but then I'm a couple of years older. Her dreadlocks gave her a defiant and youthful look. She had stayed slim and, from what I could see, was still wearing multi colored jackets. The accent was still there but with a strong, definite New York turn, I'm not sure for the best.

We first exchanged family news but mine were terse since I had remained single all these years and had no family or close relatives in my life. She gave me a brief glimpse into her own, but I couldn't help notice the lack of enthusiasm she brought to the conversation.

Somehow we talked, but I didn't feel we were communicating. I feared that time had worked its eroding magic and destroyed our friendship.

It was at least a week later when Clara left a message on my voice mail, inviting me for dinner at her house. I'm not sure why I called back and agreed, but I honestly wanted to try and recapture some of our past if at all possible.

At a time when both of us were at the bottom rung of office work, we used to enjoy happy hour with its free or nearly so drinks and all the hors-d'oeuvres you could eat between five and seven. She had children somewhere; a daughter living with an ex-husband, and a son with her mother in Jamaica, but this was not something she talked about freely.

We made a strange couple, the white, conservative-looking woman from upper New York State hanging-out with the dark exotic island beauty. Sometimes, we would sit in Central Park, bottle of wine in a brown paper bag, stealing sips whenever we felt no one was looking. Once in a while, she dared buy a joint from casual dealers hanging around, and, although this was foreign to me, I went along for the ride. This was the most excitement I had since, well, since never.

##

I arrived at her house, a small apartment in one of the recently renovated neighborhoods of Brooklyn, at around six and she handed me a glass of white wine, remembering my favorite drink. I couldn't smell dinner being cooked, but figured salad was likely on the menu... that or take-out, safely tucked in the microwave.

First thing she asked was how I fared as a psychologist in the city. I had to be honest; it was not an easy ride. I had joined a clinic earlier that year and was still struggling to develop the clientele I would need to make a decent living in this town. I often wondered why I had come back to New York. I confessed to Clara that, perhaps my years in the city as her friend, had probably been the best of my life and this is probably what brought me back.

She laughed, remembering how broke and, sometimes pathetic, we were, but this was the truth.

We had been making conversation for a bit when I finally figured out where this sadness was coming from. Her fiftieth birthday was coming up and she was reassessing her goals and ambitions. She too, thought our carefree time in the seventies had been precious and while she didn't want to relive our crazy antics, or any other ones she has lived through later, she admitted to have lost any sense of spontaneity and fun. She was bored, and, from where I sat, depressed.

And yes, that night we had take-out. Chinese, I think, and we talked until well after midnight. We decided to meet for dinner at least once or twice a month. I left excited about having found my friend again and looked forward to the next time.

##

I went through this mid-century crisis myself a 'couple' of years ago and still haven't quite figured out or maybe fully realized its effect on me. Perhaps because I have no children who flew the nest to start their own lives, perhaps because I have no husband with a mid-life crisis, or is it because of a late menopause which came with barely any of the symptoms a lot of women seem to experience? I don't know, but I somehow sailed through it unscathed. What I know is that I find it hard to deal with women and age-related problems, even as a professional.

Clara called me a week later and asked if I wanted to drop by for a drink at her apartment that night after work. My social life being almost non-existent, I was happy for the chance to see her again.

I found her place a bit messier than the last time. She sat on her well worn brown couch smoking a cigarette, impervious to me and I am wondering why she asked me over that night.

I have to apologize here if my tone is a bit too dry. I can't help but look at people, even friends, in a more intellectual and analytical fashion which is probably why, in retrospect, I don't have many friends. I'm just writing this to help me understand why women find it so hard to age. I think it may help me figure out why I have problems dealing with this issue.

"So Clara," I said, "we have to plan a big birthday party for you soon, don't we?"

She gives me a sad smile. "I don't think so." She replies, eyes on the smoke that rises slowly to the water damaged ceiling.

"Still looking for Mr. Right these days?"

She laughs, "looking for Mr. Right.? Nah. Men are too old, too fat, or too needy. Besides, have you read the papers lately? Women are found in trunks of cars, beaten, killed… nah, this woman is going to be single for a long time."

For someone who invited me over, she isn't very talkative. I remembered that we hadn't talked about her family much, at least not in details the last time we met. I jumped on the subject.

"How are the kids" I ask.

"Well, you know Louisa lives in England with Leila and Oscar." She pauses. "God, what were they thinking when they named that one? Anyway, she just got divorced. Not surprising considering her husband was never home anyway. He was also kind of creepy looking if you want to know the truth." She hesitates, "she and the kids are supposed to come down for Christmas. At least that's what Louisa told me when I was there for Easter". Clara pauses. "Marco, well, Marco is being Marco. He's still in California. He and his wife are involved in the movie business. She pauses and frowns; "did I tell you he just had a kid? Named him Winfrey." She rolls her eyes. "He's doing OK I guess. I don't see him much either." "How about Andrew?" I ask wondering if her second ex-husband ever showed up again. She gives me a sly look.

"That asshole? I haven't seen him since Marco was born. He never came back, never paid a cent for his kid and is probably out there producing more kids he can't afford. I don't care if I never see him again." She stops. "You never met him, did you?" she asks me.

"No, you just told me about him at the time."

Clara puts her cigarette out and rises from the couch. "Want a drink?" she asks.

"Sure, thanks." I feel a little uncomfortable but the wine makes things more relaxed.

She pours herself a glass of wine as well and resumes her post on the couch.

"How about your job?" I ask, knowing that she never completed her nursing degree, but is involved in some indirect way with the medical profession.

"OK. My boss is great, but you know with all the budget cuts everywhere and stuff, I always wonder how long it will be before I'm out of a job."

She lights up again and looks at me. "Did I tell you my mom died last year?" she asks.

"No, you had mentioned that she was sick in one of your Christmas cards, but I didn't realize she had passed. Did you go home to see her before she died?"

"Yes" she replies and pauses. "I sat by her bed for a week before she finally gave up. They had her drugged up so bad, she had no clue what was going on."

"What did she die of?" I ask.

"Cancer."

As women, that word always has a disturbing effect. We sit, silent for a while, perhaps looking for a definition of this word that will make us more comfortable.

"I thought you had quit smoking years ago." I say, changing the subject, although the word association was probably obvious. "I did, for a while," she replies, "but after mom died, I figured what the hell. I'm next in line to go and, really, it's not like anyone depends on me or that I have that much to live for." She makes a gesture encompassing the room and furniture then shrugs.

I always find it difficult when faced with someone whose depression seems to give them a clarity that is difficult to counter: she's right, in a way. It's even more difficult when dealing with a friend since the urge to confess that 'I've felt like that myself many times' is difficult to resist.

"I went to see Louisa for Easter." Clara said, forgetting that she had told me earlier.

"How did that go?" I ask, sensing that this event is part of the dark place where Clara is right now.

"I had a great time with the kids, we went to the park, rode the 'tube', went to the street markets..." She hesitates, "at least the first couple of days. Then they had to go back to school and between the piano lessons, French tutor, organized readings, I don't think I saw them more than an hour at breakfast everyday. Louisa works downtown, so I pretty much roamed around the city on my own most of the time. I couldn't believe how expensive it is there. I could never afford to move back." She snickers, "Anyway, I think we were all glad when I packed-up to come back home."

She continues, "Do you know how that feels when your kids only want you around just because they feel guilty otherwise? You just know they really wish you just acted the grandma without interfering with the kids' schedule and then pretty much leave them alone. It's like," she hesitates, "like they wish you were a puppet they could sit at the dinner table and move you around as required, certain that no opinions are to be voiced or family dogmas challenged." She glances at me and I nod. I have no personal experience, but I heard many versions of the same story from some of my older patients.

"See," she says, "I'm not sure what I'm supposed to do for the next fifty years. Do I start a new family?" She laughs. "The thought of taking on responsibilities like children or even volunteer work makes me shiver with dread. But, aren't we supposed to be useful at something? Can I just stop doing anything worth while and still continue living as though nothing happened?"

Clara shifts on the couch and lights up another cigarette. "Do you mind if I smoke" she finally asks.

"Clara, you know how I feel about smoking, so I can't lie and say I don't." She puts the cigarette out. "I really should quit again anyway. I've been feeling like shit lately. Louisa kept telling me how I stank the whole time I was there, so the kids started sniffing around me and sort of avoided me all together, eventually."

She shifts in her seat. "There's this woman at work," she continues, "her husband just retired and he's spending all his free time on the golf course and they go up north on weekends to fish, or sit around some rustic cottage. I can't imagine my life like this."

I can feel her unraveling.

"Did I tell you about my bum knee?" I shake my head. "Well, I may have to have a knee replacement. Can you believe that? I thought this was just for old people. Can I live in this city if I can't walk?" She is now angry. "Hell, I wish I could just pick up and leave."

"Why don't you?" I ask, knowing full well that it gets harder and harder with the years. The adventurous mind is still active, but the body won't cooperate and motivation wanes a lot faster than it used to.

She frowns and shakes her head. "Really, where would I go? How would I live? Not with my kids who, in any case, wouldn't want me around." She shifts and extends her legs out on the couch, not without an almost indiscernible wince of pain as she moves.

"Who would hire a washed up, fifty year old bummed-knee, black woman anyway? It's not like I have any savings or anything. I can't just quit my job."

Images are crossing the path of her mind's eye as I'm watching her battle with her feelings. "Really, what is left for me to do?"

"Clara," I reply, "you may have another fifty years to go. There is plenty to be done. You're a smart woman, you have plenty of experience... Did you ever think of going back to school?"

She laughs. "School, me? Hated it when I was a kid and would likely hate it now. Remember I was going to be a nurse? That lasted just long enough for me to learn that I have no patience for sick people and I do better shuffling papers in an office. Besides, it's really expensive. You can't get a break until you're a bona fide senior citizen. That's the problems: I'm too old for most things, but too young to take advantage of being old."

She turns and stares at me and continues in this low, sarcastic tone I have not heard in a long time. "Woman, I need a man. I want someone to take care of my old carcass and make a lady of leisure out of me. That's what I want. I think I'd be good at it."

"But you just said you'd be single forever." She shrugs. "Yeah, yeah. That's bullshit." She stopped and looked up at the ceiling as if searching for an answer. "I don't know. The idea of being taken care of sounds good. Then I think of dirty underwear, bad eating habits or maybe even snoring every night in my bed and I think I'm better off alone." We both laugh.

The evening continues with her surreptitiously convincing me that perhaps there is no life after fifty, especially if you're alone and with the possibility of becoming disabled. Where does that leave me?

##

I called her a week later and insisted that this time I would do the honor. Our next 'date' is in my apartment. It's hard to let go of my habitual psycho stuff, but I really now just want to help my friend through a difficult time.

She shows up, fashionably late, with a bottle of red Bordeaux and some inspirational best seller she had been reading and wants my opinion on.

I had prepared my famous chicken curry as I know Indian food is still her favorite, and baked brownies, not the ones we used to bake while giggling in the 70's, but ones rich enough to mellow the mood.

I could tell she had mellowed her own mood before coming over: the aroma of freshly smoked marijuana was hovering around her like an aura. I know she was involved with various drugs in the past, but now I realize she is still finding solace and comfort in the weed patch. It's a good way to keep from facing your feelings. In fact, I confess that I haven't 'indulged' in a long time because I'm somehow convinced that I would get caught and be thrown in jail forever. I know it makes no sense but we can't choose our own paranoia. I envy her ability to just do what she thinks is good for her.

She thumbs through the book she brought while I open the bottle of wine and we both sit on the couch facing my fake fireplace. I tell her she has to give up the pop psychology stuff: "Someone has an insight, good or bad, and goes on to write a whole book about it. The best advice I always have about those is using them to stabilize your table or bed if your floors are uneven."

I leave her to the books while I start serving dinner.

"You know, I was thinking," she starts, then hesitates. "Well, thinking is always a good sign" I smile.

"No, well, when you think of it, what would really happen if I wasn't there anymore?" She paused. "The kids would be too glad to split the insurance I have at work, they would cry for an appropriate amount of time, but really, what difference would it make in the grand scheme of things?"

I see she is serious and decide to let her pursue that thought on her own. To be honest I often feel that way myself, so who was I to contradict? "Let's just eat" I suggest.

She perks up noticeably during dinner, food and wine merging together to form the perfect interlude. We start planning an outing to see the latest play on Broadway and maybe some old fashioned 'hanging-out' time in some of the trendy bars. I'm getting excited at the prospect and at the fact that she is now talking about the future, which means that she believes there is one.

"I know," I say, "I know you don't want a party for your birthday, but I'll take you out. We'll tell everyone you're turning forty and have them convince you that you don't look a day over thirty. How does that sound?"

She laughs. "Only you could pull that off. Yes, maybe. Could be fun."

"OK, it's a date." I walk to my wall calendar and draw a large circle around her birthday.

The atmosphere is far more relaxed now and we go back to the couch for amaretto and some baklava I bought at my favorite Greek bakery.

"I have an appointment with the doctor next week." Clara says in a more serious manner".

I ask if it's about her knee.

"No, I've been feeling sort of 'off' lately and I thought I should get checked out."

"I'm sure it's nothing," I try to reassure her. Probably just a winter funk growing on you." She laughs again and rises to leave.

"And thanks for the great dinner. I'm sure it'll keep me going for a while. My place next time. You don't mind take-out do you? You may remember I'm not the best cook in town." Clara smiles and gives me a last hug before walking down to the subway.

##

She calls me the following Tuesday and asked if I can drop by later that day. "I'm home now and won't be going anywhere." She adds. The tone of her voice causes me to rearrange my schedule so I am free to meet with her as early as I can.

She looks fine when I get to her apartment and we first talk about the weather and other such topics as though nothing special is going on. Then, she falls silent.

I break the silence. "So, you said you were seeing your doctor this week. What did she say?"

She looks up, then down again at her hands, and remains silent. "Well…" I ask again.

"Let's put it this way, my knee may become the least of my worry," she starts, trying to lighten up the dark aura which had now taken over. "Seems like I have a lump in my breast. I hadn't even noticed, not that I play with myself so much," she laughs, but it's a sad grin.

"What did the doctor say?" I try to stay calm. "When are you going to find out about it?" Still avoiding my eyes, she tells me there is going to be a biopsy tomorrow.

I cancel my appointments for the next day and force my presence on Clara. This is well beyond facing a half century of life. This is facing life itself. In another time or place, I may have told her that, well, this may be what she was looking for, seeing how depressed she was, but this was much too real for light humor.

We leave the hospital together and I drive her back home. No words are exchanged. None need be. She tries to send me away but I won't leave. Here we are, two middle aged women, well if we live to be 100, that is, with nothing to loose but their lives and one of them is in the balance.

I stay with her overnight and ask my assistant to re-schedule my appointments for the next few days. She has told no one yet, waiting for the verdict to come in.

Every time the phone rings, we both hold our breaths. That fateful afternoon, it is already dark outside but we haven't turned any lights on yet. The phone rings, she jumps to her feet, forgetting about the pain shooting from her knee, but stops when she reaches the phone. "Do you want me to answer it?" I ask. She just looks at me and picks up the phone.

I see her face transformed from tired and worried to shattered and helpless. She is talking in monosyllables, but I understand the conversation.

When Clara hangs up all I can say is "When?" She sits back down. "I have to have surgery next week. The chemo starts after that."

I want to say I am sorry, but I know it's not enough. What is happening to my professional training? I feel completely overwhelmed and just nod. I stay with her until she assures me she will survive the night.

##

For the next few weeks, I cease being the friend and become the sister, even mother to this woman who had lost the ability to lean on someone else. Clara resists at first, but then becomes too weak to fight my will to care for her. I make all the calls; Louisa promises to visit as soon as possible while Marco said he is booked to come over in a short while, so he will see her then. They are both concerned and look for assurances I can't provide but yet are still unwilling to disrupt their busy lives to care for their mother.

She calls her friends and they all come to commiserate and make her feel that many people care about her. Ones she hadn't seen in ages are crawling out of the woodwork; some bringing her good wishes, others, relief from the nausea and pain.

Clara's beautiful hair starts falling out, first one tiny dreadlock at the time, then by the fistful. One morning she comes out of the bathroom with a shaved head. "Remember, I told you there was only one way to get rid of dreadlocks and it was by shaving them? I guess I just found another way." She smiles. "I look like Sade, don't I?"

She is, in fact quite beautiful even without hair; her face is tired, but still without blemishes or wrinkles and her head is perfectly formed. I tell her so. She sighs and shakes her head in disbelief.

I find it fascinating that depression is often lifted by a harsher reality one has to faced. I can see that Clara is learning to want to live again.

"Remember all that crap I was saying when we first started talking a couple of months ago? Boy, was it ever crap. You know the worst part is that sometimes I had the feeling you agreed with my ranting about how my life was meaningless." I lower my eyes. "Well," she continues, "sorry to disappoint you but I know I might die now and I'm scared shitless."

I finally have the courage to look up at her. "Well, I must confess that your talking to me about your feelings on turning fifty was difficult for me. I was there only a couple of years ago and to be honest I try to refer patients at this stage of their lives to a colleague." I pause trying to find the words that would, maybe not excuse my failing to help her, but at least explain them.

"You're right. I asked myself a lot of the same questions and, to be honest I am still asking them today. Like, what am I doing that is worth doing? You have kids, grandchildren, friends who, as you saw, really care about you. I envy you in a strange sort of way. I can't help asking myself who would care about me if I were to face what is happening to you now."

Clara comes up to give me a hug and sits next to me. "See, Clara, we always thought our friendship was based on how different we were, but now I'm finding that we were fooling ourselves. Our culture, bodies, ages, jobs and everything else may be different, but we think the same way. Our minds follow the same train of thoughts and, although we don't always end up in the same place, we usually get somewhere, and most of the time, to a better place than we were before. That's what our friendship is about. Not the differences, but the similarities."

We both fall silent for a while. "You have to be OK, Clara." I smile. "If only so you can keep telling me how my clothes don't match."

She looks up frowning, a puzzled look on her face. "What do you mean your clothes don't match?"

"Don't you remember, the first time you saw me you asked, and I quote: "What's this dress about?"

Clara laughs. "I certainly remember no such thing. Although I do say that your idea of accessorizing is different from most women."

We look at each other and understand.

"You know, she says, there is this cute anesthesiologist I met when I was in the hospital the other day and I just found out he's single."

We both laugh. "Does he have a brother?" I asked.

"I can find out." She replies with a smile.

##

5

JACKIE

Associated Press. "A mugging was averted last night in France, when an American tourist, celebrating her fiftieth birthday in Paris, apprehended a man who had tried to rip a camera off her shoulder.

In almost flawless French, Jackie Anderson of Milwaukee Wisconsin, told authorities her athletic stance should have warded off the attacker. "You'd think muggers would pick on someone less likely to defend herself." A youthful, energetic Anderson said."

"It would be just like me to say something so stupid," Jackie thought, while viciously pedaling on her stationary bicycle, daydreaming about her upcoming trip.

The television set purchased last year at a yard sale for ten dollars had died that morning and all that was left to motivate her to pedal in this dreary, windowless basement was her own imagination.

"Only eight pounds to go," she muttered to herself. Eight pounds and she would look just like she did at twenty, "that is if you didn't count the wrinkles and high cheekbones which were now at chin level," she thought. Her hair was now shoulder length and, with some help from L'Oreal, had recovered a semblance of its natural auburn shade.

She quickly glanced at the reflection staring back at her from the old mirror leaning against the grey cement wall and wondered what had happened to her life. The middle aged 'sweat bag' she saw had grown out of fear of failing the children. In the process she had lost herself, her dreams and her independence.

Peter, her husband of almost 15 years, had been good to her, but now was time to assess the status of the old wings she used to soar on, in the early years. She had given up too much. She had taken too much from him. Jackie had to find out who she was and where she was going.

With her fiftieth birthday around the corner and the children grown, educated and independent, this seemed like as good a time as any to do this.

"No one plans beyond fifty", she had explained to her concerned husband, "I lived my life as though I would not have to live past the children's college years. I have to find out what I'm supposed to do now."

She'd left out the desperation part and the increased depression she felt would destroy what was left of her, if kept unchecked. She had mastered the art of keeping up appearances, so no one suspected the turmoil that was going on inside her head. She had to do something and this was it.

Her parents, retired in Arizona, and the kids, both on a budding career path, wouldn't even notice she was gone. Whatever friends she had, if you could call them friends, didn't understand why she wanted to leave her 'charmed' life, risking losing her husband, not to mention the possible dangers involved in such an adventure.

These were not real friends: all they saw was what Jackie allowed them to see, a happy, sometimes even exuberant woman who 'had it all'. She had only ever confided her fears and insecurities to Janice, her age-old buddy from New York. She had avoided all local acquaintances lately. She didn't plan to see them until she returned… "If I return." She muttered surprised by this thought which was surfacing for the first time.

She thought about her next door neighbor. Jackie had never spoken to the woman but had heard that her husband had just left, trading her for a younger model. Now, the woman had lost so much weight as to appear anorexic. She also had a different man as well as a permanent glass of wine in her hand every time Jackie caught sight of her on the backyard deck adjacent to the fence that separated the two properties. In spite of this woman being a relative stranger, Jackie could see the rapid path to self-destruction she was on. Neighbors who used to occasionally visit her were now avoiding her presence as though her fate was contagious. Jackie decided she never wanted to become so pathetic.

Still pedaling, she shrugged these negative thoughts away, and smiled as she remembered the plane tickets, one an open return voucher, safely tucked in her passport.

The flawless French part of the imaginary press release bothered her. With the TV on the blink, she made up her mind to splurge on the expensive set of French lessons on CD's she had been eyeing every time she went for coffee at Barnes and Nobles on 76th. She could listen to the discs on her portable player while doing her workout or running.

A timer prompted her to get off the stationary bike. She would normally workout to her favorite aerobics tape but, without the TV, it was impossible, so she decided to go for a short run around the park.

Her free weights were beckoning, the unwritten rule being that no true workout was complete without them, but she decided they'd have to wait. Smiling at her own clever pun, she traded the tennis shoes she preferred to cycle in for her running shoes.

Gathering her thoughts while stretching, Jackie wondered what new adventure she would dream up while running. In the last few years, she had become very adept at fantasy. Her life, as seen by the outside world, was a series of successes and accomplishments. But what everyone saw was a designer version of her life that bore no resemblance to her reality.

She knew Peter was aware of her made-up world, but went along with it for fear that she would abandon him. He didn't suspect that she had lost the flame that used to spark her whimsical flights and that even now, on the eve of this adventure; she often had second thoughts and feared the unknown. Jackie had built a mental stone wall to block out depression and had the ability to squash any type of rebellious feelings down to an art.

Lately, however, with her imminent mid century birthday, her guards were weakening and she couldn't hold the demons at bay anymore.

Hunger pangs were luring her to the kitchen, but considering the last few pounds yet to be shed, she decided that she'd have to live with them until lunch. "Who said exercising cuts down appetite?" She wondered and started her jog, mentally composing an article for an imaginary fitness magazine on that very subject.

The emotional roller coaster was in motion. Jackie was aware of its existence, it wasn't her first ride, but she couldn't turn the off key that would have given her the peace she so yearned for. Escape seemed to be the only way to stop or at least muffle its thunderous flight.

O'Hare was bustling with traffic on this sunny September afternoon. The Air France flight wouldn't leave until evening, but Jackie had wanted to be there early and, to silence her guilt, share one last dinner with her husband. She had said goodbye to the girls earlier, assuring them that the long drive to see her off was not necessary.

The ride to the airport had been heavy with silence. Peter had also been quiet through the dinner, still unsure of Jackie's motive for leaving and whether it had anything to do with him. She could only convey that this was something she had to do, but offered no guarantees or promises.

Although everyone thought she was a strong, decisive women who made most of the decisions in the marriage and family, this trip was, in fact, the first original choice she had made in almost fifteen years and she would go through with it, if only to prove to herself that she still could have a life outside the family.

She had butterflies rising up and down her body like so many emotional yoyos. Jackie often traveled alone, but this time was different. There were no relatives or old friends to visit. There was only a strong determination Peter could see every time he caught her eyes; it was a look he had not seen in years and feared. Jackie was purposely projecting this image so she could safely hide her own doubts and fears from him. If he had known, he may have convinced her to stay, and that, she could not face.

Jackie watched Peter carry her luggage to the airline counter. He was still handsome. His blond hair was now darker with a few gray threads, but his body still had the trim look of the man she had met sixteen years earlier. As for him, he hadn't even noticed her new figure, her trendy pony tail or the fact that she had traded her old stirrup pants and loose fitting shirt for a new pair of tight jeans and sweater.

In a way, she didn't mind his lack of concern for her looks since it meant he probably didn't even notice age taking hold of her body. The jeans may have been a mistake on such a long flight, she thought, but the figure reflected in a shop window told her it was worth the discomfort. She smiled, the roller coaster rising up a new hill.

Peter's love was unconditional, but Jackie often wondered if he wasn't in love with the idea of her as a nurturer and a friend rather than a human being in her own rights. "He would give me the world if he could," she thought, "but basically knows nothing about me." He never saw beneath the surface and hoped she would let him know if something was wrong. She never did or if she attempted to, he would change the subject. He would also go to his workshop, or turn on his computer whenever he saw a sad or weary look on her face. He had no close friends and relied on Jackie for all their social activities. She often thought he would be lost without her and that, in itself, made her angry: this was what tied her down to this life, the guilt of causing pain to her husband. Can a whole relationship be based on guilt?

Peter pulled Jackie towards him for one last hug before she crossed the point of no return. She hoped he wouldn't linger at the gate as she was mentally ready for this solo flight and was anxious to take off. "I love you." he said.

She hated that. He knew she was uncomfortable with the L word. Why now? Their physical relationship was flimsy at best and had they not been friends, they may have gone their separate ways a long time ago. She could barely respond with a weak 'I love you too' and proceed to the gate.

##

Jackie was sitting in a restaurant, her sister across from her and a handsome young man at her side. The man was obviously interested in her and she loved the attention. No man had looked at her like that in a long time, and although she knew she should stop right there, the attraction was too great.

She was trying to concentrate on her sister's conversation, but had no clue what she was talking about. Then she turned to her companion and found he had turned into a shriveled old man, a flash fire consuming his face.

Jumping up in her seat, heart pounding in her chest, Jackie realized she had been awakened by the sun peaking over the airplane wing. She glanced at her watch. Three thirty. She shook the cob webs from her brain remembering her destination and realizing she was flying into a ready-made day. Her chest tightened as the dream surged back in her mind.

Of course the woman sitting across from her in the restaurant was Kathy, her daughter: she always perceived her as a sister in her dreams. She never dreamed about her actual sister whom she visited once a year so they could both brag about their lives but never really communicating since they had nothing in common. The man's transformation in her dream somehow didn't change the fact that for a short moment, she had recaptured this 'being wanted' feeling which had been missing from her life for more years than she cared to remember. She briefly hugged herself and shivered.

Watching the sun across the horizon, listening to the silent hum of the engine, panic slowly oozed itself into her consciousness. She looked at the man beside her and considered an accidental shove to wake him, start a conversation and hence bring her self back to the real world. Years of propriety, however, won against the urge to communicate and she leaned back in her seat.

The skies above and the ocean below were calm and immaculate. "What if the plane was upside down, she thought as she looked up, this could be the ocean."

The very thought made her nauseous. She closed her eyes and tried to concentrate on what she would do when she arrived at Charles de Gaulle.

"Votre passeport s'il vous plaît." Commanded a little mustached Frenchman from behind the counter. Visions of Agatha Christie's Hercule Poirot undercover caused Jackie to smile to herself.

"Vous n'avez pas indiqué le nom de votre hôtel sur la formule de douanes." He continued.

"Ah non? Hôtel Les Grandes Ecoles dans St. Germain." She countered, wondering how she could have forgotten to write the hotel name when all she had done was to stare at this silly customs form for an hour before landing. Her expensive French lessons were already paying off and for that she was grateful.

The agent stamped her passport and motioned her through.

Jackie walked out of customs, one bag on her shoulder, the other on her back, trying to decide which way to exit when she was startled by a light tap on her shoulder. In the semi-fog of the time lapse she was finding herself into, she turned to face a man obviously wanting her attention.

"I'm sorry, I just heard you tell the agent that your hotel was in St. Germain, he said. So is mine. Would you like to share a cab?"

Jackie had thought of using the metro for her first taste of the city, but she could only stare at the man. She had vaguely noticed him in the first class section when boarding in Chicago.

"My name is Josh Arnold, he said extending his free hand while rearranging his luggage with the other. I heard you with the customs man and your French would really help me deal with the driver. They're worse than New York cabbies." He smiled and stopped to assess Jackie's hesitation.

"I don't know, she said, taking his hand by reflex, I thought I'd use the subway..." She looked around half expecting someone to rescue her from this conversation.

"I could use the company and since I need you for translation the ride is on me, that is if we both successfully get to our destination."

"Well," Jackie's thoughts hovered between the excitement of the metro, this man's request and the fact that any kind of savings would be welcome on this odyssey. He looked harmless enough and adventure was what this trip was all about. What the hell. "All right. I'm Jackie," she said, extending her own hand again in agreement. "I'll try to help you out if I can."

Jackie followed her new acquaintance to the taxi area where a driver casually mixed their bags at random in the trunk, assuming some intimacy between the passengers.

She rushed her instructions in French in an attempt to fool the fellow into believing she was a native. She might have enjoyed a 'grand tour' considering she wasn't paying, but she assumed her cab-mate would not appreciate it after such a long flight.

She knew when he acknowledged her in English that it hadn't worked. At least she wouldn't have to pretend any longer and could take advantage of the ride to find out more about her companion, now comfortably installed in the comparatively luxurious Mercedes back seat.

"Their cabs are certainly a step above American standards," was all she thought of saying. He nodded in assent and turned his head to stare out his window. She sighed, resigned to stay in her corner and wondered if this is how all her so-called adventures in Paris would go? This wasn't a good sign.

Taking a closer look at the man, she quickly realized she was dealing with someone who looked at least ten years her junior, and was also quite attractive. Not her type however. Men like this one never were attracted to her and, until now, vice versa.

A dark curl on his forehead was the only witness to the long flight and served to accentuate the classic, but still somewhat boyish features. The shadow on his cheeks and chin attested to the day they'd left behind and reminded her of how unprepared she was for this one. He was sporting a designer, but casual, layered outfit with loafers that looked custom designed to complete the look.

Suddenly conscious of her own department store jeans and jacket, Jackie shrank back in her seat and was suddenly taken back to a childhood memory at home with her family.

##

"You're not going out like this." Debbie, her older sister would say.

Jackie was 14 and just wanting to hang with her friends at the diner. "Why, what's wrong?" She asked back, suddenly subdued, as though she didn't already know. "Nothing in your outfit matches. Are you colorblind?" And, giving her sister a disgusted look-over, Debbie would deliver the final blow. "That pony tail just has to go."

For an hour, Jackie would allow her sister to 'fix her up' as she put it and eventually leave the house, hair in a tight bun, uncomfortable in her sister's trendy clothes, all wind out of her sails, feeling ugly and inadequate, but stylish.

##

Since living in Wisconsin, appropriate wardrobe had thankfully not been an issue. But the feeling lingered and Jackie decided this was going to be a long taxi ride.

"If you were to wake up in a cab leaving an airport almost anywhere in the world, you wouldn't have a clue of where you are." He said, almost to himself.

Shocked to hear him talk, she turned her head, just in time to see that he must have been looking at her while she was reminiscing and hoped she hadn't

174

grimaced or muttered to herself as was her incurable habit.

"Airports all do look the same." she replied, bored by her own platitude.

Their eyes locked for a brief moment. She felt her insides shift and, if she had been prone to blushing, this would have been one of those times.

Visions of past adventures, some in less comfortable, but anonymous New York's yellow cabs came to the surface and the memory brought moist beads forming on her forehead. "Great she thought, I'm in Paris, in a cab with a handsome man and I'm sweating."

She thankfully noticed that it was, in fact, quite warm in the car, so her thoughts only accounted for part of the heat and it wasn't the beginning of the dreaded, but not yet experienced, hot flash.

Josh was now busy removing his jacket and she decided that was a good idea. She removed her own as delicately as was possible in such confined quarters, a bit self conscious about the sweater, now clinging to her body.

"Have you been to Paris before?" he asked.

"A long time ago, she lied. I'm sure it's changed a lot since then."

"Paris is always Paris. Unless you look in the suburbs and see the tall modern buildings, I'd say it probably hasn't changed much since the revolution or, at best the world fair."

Afraid of having to make up some story about a previous visit, she tried to encourage his monologue. "How often do you come here?"

"Oh, I've been coming on business for the last couple of years; this must be my fifth visit." He smiled. "You'd think I'd speak some French by now" and he glanced quickly at her, "or, I'd have found some sexy French woman to interpret for me. I only come for a couple of days at the time to attend meetings, so, I guess I'm one of those 'ugly Americans'. I expect everyone to learn English and I'm not in the least interested in other cultures."

Disappointed in such a closed minded attitude, she wondered if this conversation was worth pursuing. There were enough mindless rednecks back home, she didn't need the hassle of one with thousand dollar shoes.

She thought she spotted Sacré-Coeur rising on the left of the highway, but her doubts would have evidenced her earlier lie, so she decided to keep her comments to herself.

Benign conversation continued throughout the trip, mostly one-sided on his part, and she saw by the street names, which she had thoroughly studied on city maps in the planning stage of her escape, that they were finally nearing her destination.

Part of her wanted to prolong the trip, but the more logical part of her brain told her this was ludicrous. Besides, she wanted to meet Paris, not some pedantic, self-centered American from Chicago.

From the look on the driver's face, he was none too pleased when she told him only she would be leaving and he was to sort out the luggage and drive the Monsieur to his hotel.

The stranger turned to her and handed his business card. A note was written on the back. He explained, "this is where I'll be staying while in Paris. I'm only here for the weekend, but if you want to go out, or need anything, just leave a message at the hotel." She lowered her eyes to scan the information and the cab was gone before she raised her head again. Joshua Arnold, the card read, International Marketing Consultant.

Looking around her, she saw that a coach door, opening unto a courtyard bore the name of her hotel. Finally assessing her position, she took a deep breath, looked up at the early afternoon sun and walked in looking as self-assured as she could under the circumstances.

##

Registration was painless and, her bags unpacked, she leered at the bed, mentally computing the time zone and concluding that people at home were still sleeping while she had been up for nearly 24 hours. Jackie felt that the time sleeping in the plane didn't count. "No," she thought, "I'm not giving in."

"The worst thing you can do for jet lag," her old New York girlfriend Janice had said, "is to have a nap when you get there." Heeding the advice, Jackie quickly grabbed her wallet, stuffed it in her jeans' hip pocket and, armed only with a room key and her weariness, she left the room.

The sun was hot considering the late September date, and some guests were drinking wine or aperitifs in the courtyard, gathered around artistically arranged patio tables, exchanging pleasantries with each other.

Jackie spotted a couple, contemporaries, who were 'holding court' and seemed to know everyone walking in and out of the hotel.

He, with the long graying hair and bandana, she, with jeans and tie-dye shirt, Jackie secretly wished her life could have stopped at the time when she too was a carefree soul.

"Get back in the car." Tommy said. "Make me." Jackie laughed, using the beat-up VW beetle as a shield. Stop fooling around or we'll never make it to Woodstock."

They had stopped again so she could use the rest room in a gas station, the third pit stop since leaving at five that morning. "You're no fun." She brooded, back inside the car. "Do you think we can do the last twenty miles without stopping again?" He asked, growing impatient.

"Sorry, I'm just so nervous, and I've had all that coffee this morning." She lied. She was nervous, but for a different reason. Her period was late and she'd have to wait a few days before finding out if she was in fact pregnant.

Jackie sat back in her seat and tried to relax while brushing sweat from her forehead; she pondered at what life would be like as a housewife, married to an insurance man. He was 22 years old and had a good job. She had graduated high school last year and worked for her dad in his accounting firm. Marriage wasn't something they had talked about. It was scary, but if she was pregnant, there was no alternative in her mind. This was 1969 and that's what proper people did.

For now, she noticed him looking at her sideways and wondered what was on his mind, then dozed off until they reached their destination.

Surrounded by music, love and peace signs, elated from the atmosphere of friendship and togetherness, Jackie revealed her secret suspicions to Tommy.

That weekend, spent in a daze of music, lovemaking, marijuana and cheap wine was to be the last carefree one in a long line of days spent writing invitations, registering for gifts to prepare for the inevitable wedding.

Kathy was born that winter and Stephanie followed less than two years later.

It was only when the divorce came through almost ten years later that she found out that Tommy had planned to break up with her on that historical weekend. He had been investigating going back to school under the GI Bill and had just received an acceptance notice from UCLA. Instead, they had settled down in a small house, courtesy of her parents and Tommy became one of the youngest claims clerk to make supervisor in the history of the insurance company where he had worked since coming back from the navy.

##

Jackie moved back to the present and her brain, already confused by the loss of sleep, took-in the unusual couple and struggled to find its way back to this bright September day in Paris. She walked out of the garden. Every second shop seemed filled with pastries, cheeses and cuts of meats she'd never seen before, or if she had, they never looked quite this appealing.

The four cafés framing the square nearest to the hotel beckoned for her to stop. Le Shoppe, she read above the one she was most attracted to. She self-consciously sat on the tiny round chair but quickly checked herself and adopted her long lost "I'm alone and it's OK look", she had learned to plaster on her face from the days in the late seventies when bars were the only places where she could pretend to be anyone she wanted and hopefully seduce some unsuspecting guy, if only he rated a 10.

"It's like riding a bicycle," she thought, "you never forget."

"Une petite carafe de vin rouge s'il vous plaît." She asked the passing waiter and, glancing at the menu board hanging on a column near the entrance she added "et aussi un croque-monsieur." The waiter nodded, smiled and went back inside.

She hadn't had a croque-monsieur since her visit to Montréal with Peter and the kids five years before.

To the naked eye, it looked like a ham and cheese sandwich, but the connoisseur knew it was a luncheon delicacy. Her mouth watered at the though and she wondered where the name, meaning 'bite-mister' came from.

Pleased with her French and by the fact that she was successfully blending in with the midday crowd, she sat back, smiled and enjoyed watching the old stone fountain in the square and the various scenarios that played out around its boundaries.

The waiter arrived with a full carafe of Beaujolais, and she realized she'd have to drink it or explain that she only wanted a little carafe, a quarter or half liter, not a full one. "What the hell. I have time," she thought. "Merci" she smiled up at the waiter, watching him set up the utensils and condiments on the tiny café table for her upcoming lunch. She leaned back, enjoying her first sip of wine on the continent, and using the drink to shed a first layer of guilt.

Scooters parked against the fence around the fountain reminded Jackie of her first visit to Bermuda. "These were the best of times, she thought, these were the worst of times."

It was 1974 when Jackie and Tommy arrived in Bermuda where, after five years of marriage, they planned to have the honeymoon that never was. Their respective parents agreed to share custody of the kids for a week and they landed in the middle of the country's annual Cup Match, four day weekend celebration.

Neither had ever been to a resort island and the heavily flower-scented humidity that welcomed them when stepping out of the plane overwhelmed their senses. Customs were cleared efficiently, and the couple came out looking for the shuttle bus which would take them to the seaside hotel where they were to spend one of the most exciting weeks since Woodstock.

Ignoring the pool and welcoming party, they aimed for the ocean. Scooters, mopeds and bicycles were vying for space on the narrow lanes leading to the beach. A somewhat orderly confusion reigned throughout the island as the annual, sometimes never ending, cricket match took place.

They spent two days roaming the 30 miles of islands by moped, one day walking the railroad trail, another drinking Rum Swizzle's by the pool and getting languorously wasted. A couple of quick shopping trips to Hamilton, one by ferry, the other by foot to buy duty free souvenirs for the family and it was over. He gave her a new wedding ring for their fifth anniversary, promised a return trip on their tenth. Neither knew this would never come to pass.

The server came with her croque-monsieur, snapping her out of the reverie. She tried to concentrate on what was going on in the present, but the wine, teamed with the new taste sensation of the sandwich kept her mind in a cloudy place where neither time nor space counted.

By the time all was consumed, it was well into the afternoon and she decided to punish her body for another three hours, and then reward her efforts with some well deserved sleep.

Jackie walked around the area for a while, in awe of the extraordinary architecture and the well groomed gardens that were an integral part of the buildings. By the time she was once again facing the portal to her hotel, it was almost dark.

She noticed the same couple having wine, but sitting at a different table. The woman smiled at her; Jackie decided to prolong her agony and stop by their table. She had been silent too long and needed the company.

They seemed eager to start a conversation. "What a beautiful evening." Jackie started, surmising from their previous demeanor that they welcomed any conversation from fellow residents.

"Is this your first time at Les Grandes Ecoles?" The woman asked.

"Yes. I just got here today and I'm trying to last until at least nine before going to sleep."

"It's a good idea." Nodded the man who introduced himself as Richard and pointed to his companion

"Nancy always stays up for two days when we travel. I'm not sure it does any good, but it seems to work for her."

His smile was one of intimacy and Jackie felt a pang of jealousy. She and Peter didn't share that kind of physical alliance. "Would you like to sit down and join us for a glass of wine?"

"Sure, thanks, although I've already had my share!" Jackie laughed, recounting her wine-soaked lunch earlier. Is this your first time here?" She continued, while settling down across from the couple.

"No, we've been coming here for two weeks every year for at least seven or eight years, the man said."

He then explained that he taught French in some college in Maine and his wife was an artist who produced sculptures and bas-reliefs for renovated or restored buildings.

"We've never been very good at making money, and whatever we make we spend on traveling whenever we can get away."

They were fascinating to Jackie who had begun to believe there was no one left who did what they enjoyed rather than concentrate on making more money.

The conversation went on about cold winters, the frigid waters of Ogunquit and Old Orchard beaches, even in the summer, and the carefree lifestyle all of it afforded to this couple, a pair of lovers stuck in a moment in time that had been the sixties.

Part of Jackie wanted to go back and share their lifestyle; part of her wanted to move on to new experiences, but, now, in Paris, in September, facing her fiftieth birthday, she didn't know which part would win. This is why she was here; this is what she had come to find out.

When Jackie opened her eyes the next morning, the mind-fogging jet lag was apparently beaten. The rest of her body, however, was still uncertain as to which meal it was hungry for or when or which grooming rituals should be performed.

Looking at her travel clock, she saw it was quarter after seven and wavered between a short run and a long breakfast. Food won. Breakfast at the hotel was expensive and she had to be thrifty, but she shrugged it off, deciding that this was, after all, her first 'real' day in Paris and she should treat herself. Lunch would just have to go. She was determined not to use the credit card Peter had urged her to take in case of emergency. He had financially contributed enough to her life already. She had to do this on her own.

She quickly showered, dressed in what she imagined was non-tourist-like pants and shirt, replaced her usual running shoes with black Easy Spirit casuals and walked across the courtyard to the hotel dining room.

She wanted to practice her French before venturing forth on this exploratory day and the wait staff was willing to accommodate. Weather pleasantries were exchanged and, filled with buttery croissants, strong, syrup-like coffee and rolls, she trotted through the coach door and turned left, starting up the street with determination, though she had no idea where she was going.

Her feet and instinct brought her to the Seine where she could see Notre Dame de Paris with Gargoyles guarding its flanks on the Ile de la Cité. In spite of the early hour, tourist busses were lined up on the side streets. The way one could hear German mixed with Swedish, Italian, French and English, world peace seemed possible on these ancient sacred grounds.

Shops were already open and cafés were catering to the visiting and soon-to-be-working crowd.

Stairs leading down to the walk along the river banks bore signs that the bateaux-mouches were anchored close by. Jackie would have liked to get a look the city from a different angle, but unfortunately there were no departures until ten, which meant over an hour wait. Waiting would mean having to think and it was too early to get the solace she seemed to have found in the local wine.

She climbed back up and a look at Notre Dame removed all plans of a boat tour. She walked over to the church where a service was taking place. Vivid images of past devotions came back to Jackie. Raised Catholic, churches had been a source of inspiration for most of her childhood years.

At ten, all she had to do was walk into the hundred year old chapel at the convent near her home and every hair on her body would rise to attention. She felt possessed by the Holy Spirit and communicated directly with God.

Those were the days when one of her religious teachers had suggested that a saintly vocation should perhaps be part of her future. She smiled to herself imagining what Mother Superior would have thought if she had known of her secret crush on the school chaplain. Boys were far too important to Jackie, even at that age. Also, the guilty feelings associated with them were exciting enough to keep her away from any deeper religious involvement. She had given up on her faith all together after high school and, until today, had never looked back.

She almost stopped to light a votive candle, if only to mark her reverence for this magnificently stained glassed monument to continuity, but decided it would be hypocritical, considering she had no feeling of God's presence. She would have liked to feel that presence at that moment, but her heart was empty. Perhaps a climb up to the steeples will bring some memories of God back, she thought.

Jackie paid her fare and started climbing. Grateful for the breakfast and the countless number of miles she had cycled and ran, over the last few months, she made it to the top, stopping only to look through the occasional window, carved through the rocks, displaying a preview of the vision she could expect once at the end of the upward trail.

Nothing. She felt nothing, except the awe at contemplating how, not so long ago, in a cosmic sense, beggars had climbed these steps asking the resident monks for handouts and a place to rest. The stone steps were worn down and the feeling of time-space confusion came upon Jackie once more.

She was disappointed to see that the top cat walks were surrounded by heavy metal bars which had been erected apparently to keep suicide minded visitors from jumping and injuring passers-by on the sidewalk below. She had never been suicidal, but the thought of ending it all falling from Notre Dame was strangely intriguing.

She shook her head to rid it herself of such depressing thoughts and concentrated on experiencing the almost physical excitement rising from the city. She vowed to see it all before... Well, she hadn't decided on that yet.

She climbed down and, following a couple of students whose laughter and carefree style were comforting, Jackie found herself walking back to the left bank and toward the Eiffel Tower. She could see the metal peek occasionally raising its head above the long rows of traditional six or seven story houses. The students eventually went in a different direction, but Jackie kept following this trail.

At the foot of the tower, hundreds of tourists were already lined-up to view Paris from its highest point which meant a two hour wait for the elevator.

Unwilling to hang around, Jackie decided to climb the narrow stairs as high as authorities would allow to see how far she'd get. For some reason, this metal structure did not feel part of her pilgrimage. Her brain was taking in the layout of Paris from that vantage point, but her heart wasn't in it. She wanted to see the soul behind the city, the descendants of the revolution and the whole French culture all from behind a comfortable wall of wine and pastries.

Forgetting about her previous intention of skipping lunch, she thought it was probably time to put a glaze over the darker part of her brain and block any thoughts of fear, guilt or home.

Jackie came back down the stairs, crossed a bridge, aiming for the right bank and the Champs Elysées with its wide sidewalks and trendy shops. Listening to the people around her, she discovered that Paris shoppers on a Saturday were mostly from somewhere else. It was already lunchtime so she found a café, ordered wine, a small appetizer and let her mind float above the crowd to that fuzzy new place where Jackie was happy.

It was well into the afternoon hours when she started aiming back for the hotel. She walked through a park along the Louvres which she found surrounded by trendy art galleries and antique dealers, then crossed back to the left bank. It was getting dark and she doubted her legs would carry her back to the hotel.

For a moment, she remembered who she was and why she was here, so, walking up St. Denis, she stopped to buy a cheap bottle of wine and the least expensive bottled water she could find.

She eyed the young, trendy Parisians, many of whom were munching on bread baguettes filled with paté, considered this food option but managed to resist the temptation. She just wanted to drink and sleep.

It was totally dark by the time she crossed the coach door. She was really looking forward to relaxing with her bottle of wine in the courtyard, perhaps catching the 'hippy' couple again and just chill, on this surprisingly warm autumn night.

She started towards the hotel door when her eyes caught a somewhat familiar figure sitting at the corner table, close to the flower beds. Her first reaction was to pretend she hadn't seen him, but too late. He was already on his feet with a smile plastered on his face, a rose in hand. "What are you doing here?" She asked.

"My business dinner date canceled out and I thought I'd look you up and see if you'd like to have company tonight. I was counting on your coming back to your hotel before dinner." A dapper, elegant Josh declared, handing her the rose.

Jackie self-consciously imagined what she must have looked like after ferreting all day. At a total loss for words, she took the flower, ascertained its scent, thought of how presumptuous the man was, hesitated, started to protest, but too late. He had already taken over.

"It's all set then. I've made reservations for eight thirty." "Well" Jackie finally managed to utter. "I don't know... I can't go like this" "That's all right; I'll wait for you to freshen up. I thought I could have a glass of wine while waiting, but they tell me this place is strictly 'bring your own'."

She unconsciously handed him the bottle she'd been carrying, then realizing her mistake, withdrew the gesture as quickly as she had made it. He most likely did not drink cheap grocery store wine. "I'll be right back."

She wondered why she had agreed to this. Jackie, whom everyone thought as the ultimate control freak, the ultimate 'decider', wondered if all that was just appearances; maybe her strength was only a façade to disguise her insecurities. She tried to imagine how her life would have played out if the men in her life had been so forceful and decisive.

In the meantime, she realized that her entire traveling wardrobe did not include a single designer outfit. She dug up the dressiest pants she could find, her newest turtle neck and hoped that the expensive ultra suede fitted jacket she had splurged on at Marshall Fields would carry her through. Shutting out the voice of reason in her head, she opened the wine bottle and quickly drank a glass to silence her brain.

Jackie glanced in the mirror and asked herself once more what the hell she was getting into. She shrugged and went back downstairs to join Josh. After all, what could happen?

They walked over to the Rue des Ecoles and he directed her into a small Italian Bistro where they were seated immediately.

A bottle of wine on the table, and two glasses later, Jackie assessed the situation and concluded that this was a good idea. She could never afford this restaurant and she should eat. Josh had been attentive and now that she was more relaxed, she was actually having a good time. The inner voices were quiet and the only woman left at the table was the Jackie that used to take clients out to dinner and assess the man's potential in bed.

"So, she pointedly inquired, do you have a family back home?" Josh shook his head and smiled. "This is Paris, Jackie, home doesn't exist. There's just today and tomorrow, a short meeting Monday morning and then I'm off again. Tell me, will you be spending Sunday alone?"

"Well, she smiled for what seemed to be the first time, tomorrow is actually my birthday and I thought I'd try to find something different to do."

"Great. I thought I'd visit Jim Morrison's grave at the Père Lachaise it'd be a great place to celebrate your birthday."

She noticed he had not asked for her age. "Aren't you assuming a lot here?"

"No. I just always get my way, so you have to say yes. Besides, it's in a part of town where you shouldn't go by yourself anyway, and your birthday should be celebrated surrounded by famous people.

They're being dead, is only a small annoyance." His smile had become more flirtatious and now that Jackie noticed the second bottle of wine being served, she was quite enjoying it. Her mood lightened up and the food just came and went as smoothly as the evening was progressing.

The conversation finally veered to music and literature, two subjects she was a bit more comfortable with, especially now that her guards were down.

Mentally and now physically stimulated by the conversation, the delicate food and the torrent of ideas and thoughts she had been allowed to express without restraints and sarcasm, she was glowing with excitement, anticipation and wished that this night would last forever.

Josh helped her with the jacket she couldn't remember taking off and they left the restaurant, walking briskly in the now cooler night.

He was talking, but she had no idea whether she was responding to the conversation or just rode on his words. Floating on a cloud, she watched herself, arm in arm with this man, having no clue as to their destination. It was like watching a video of herself and the only emotion she felt was one of curiosity.

Her rational mind assumed he was walking her back to the hotel, and she was surprised to find herself entering another building and following him into a strange elevator. The place was quietly stylish with gold, ornate trim, marble statues in the corner and velvet drapes in the hall windows. It was also dramatically silent, save for the occasional room service clatter heard from down the hall.

He opened a door and before she could consider her situation, she found herself in his bed, too weak to react, feeling too good to care to. She resisted for a second but finally gave up this futile attempt at thinking. "To be wanted again." This was her final thought before she finally fell asleep.

Their love making had been quick and passionate. Both were simply concentrating on their own needs, his to consummate a Paris adventure, hers to feel free to enjoy the power of a man who wanted her without any strings attached.

Jackie woke up on Sunday morning and, at first, thought she was back at home with Peter sleeping at her side. She then remembered and a wave of guilt, mixed with fear and excitement made her crawl out of bed quietly, ready to run out of this room as fast as she could. She panicked at the thought of having rushed into this unprotected affair, and, strangely enough felt relief at the sight of an obviously used condom by the bedside.

Josh stirred in his sleep and the sheet which had covered him to the waist was now loosely draped on his hip. She no longer had the excuse of too much wine or the romantic Paris evening magic.

In spite of a slight headache, it was her logical mind that was convincing her that to leave now would not make up for what had happened the night before. "Did Eve eat the entire apple?" She wondered, reasoning that if you're going to be banned from Eden for one bite, you may as well eat the whole thing. She was also basking in the 'afterglow' of the previous night and did not want to give it up yet.

The second she took to ask herself whether he would still want her today was interrupted by a sleeping hand, seemingly reaching for her where she had been sleeping only moments ago.

Sneaking back into bed, she closed her eyes, and pretended to be asleep when he reached out for her again.

Josh was now fully awake and the lovemaking was slow, almost tender, compared to the previous night's desperate passion. Jackie had not felt so excited in years.

An hour later, exhausted but relaxed, he smiled at her, not the adoring smile she was used to with Peter, but the sarcastic grin of someone who just did some mischief. In tacit assent, they went back to sleep.

Jackie woke up again at noon, quietly slipped out of bed, quickly showered and, wrapped in a towel, walked back in the room. She saw that Josh was also awake, cocked on one elbow, smiling in her general direction.

"I should go." She said, more as a question than a statement. She feared he would realize that their earlier impulsive behavior was ludicrous and, remembering her age and the subtle creases in her body, she wondered how it could have all happened. She especially cringed, thinking about her face falling off the cheek bones when she was facing down, or at the idea of his spotting one of the occasional black hair that had recently found itself on her breasts.

He looked at her, his now familiar smirk plastered on his tired, but still handsome face. "Happy Birthday, girl." He smiled, grabbed her arm and pulled her down onto the bed again.

Jackie wanted to protest, talk about her now weary clothes piled up on the floor, but she found herself melting under his gaze. She weakly attempted to break his grasp. He felt her reluctance and touched her face with the tip of his fingers. "You're really beautiful." He whispered. She smiled, her inhibitions still alive, but fading to the back of her mind. It had been oh such a long time.

She finally relaxed, remembering she was in Paris and who cared? This time their lovemaking

198

almost had a sense of caring, not of love, but of a tender intimacy which hadn't part of her marriage for years. She'd forgotten the feeling even existed or that she was still capable of experiencing it.

They may well have stayed there all day but, it was now well passed one o'clock and, as much as Jackie hated to admitted, she was starving.

Looking at yesterday's discarded clothes, she had mixed feelings about the upcoming afternoon. Sensing her discomfort, he asked "Do you want to drop by your hotel to change?" She stood back, wondering if this was a polite way of dismissing her, then seeing genuine concern in his eyes, considered the possibility. The thought, however, of seeing her own things, although she had only been staying at that hotel for 2 days, made her feel like this would bring her dangerously back to some reality she wanted to avoid.

"I know, he said, sensing her hesitation and jumping up to search through his garment bag, here's a shirt that would match your pants."

The obviously expensive silk was so soft, Jackie thought of skin as the closest thing to it. Josh gently rolled the sleeves for her and she let herself feel the luxury of the fabric on her body before wondering about yesterday's underwear lying on the floor.

He was now rummaging through his travel bag and brandished an attractive pair of bikini underwear, no doubt designed for a man, but still suitable for a woman, given the emergency.

She smiled at his anticipating her wishes, and finished dressing.

They left the room and she noticed how much larger and more luxurious his hotel was compared to hers, but somehow Les Grandes Ecoles was more what she needed right now.

Crossing to the right bank, the taxi went up the Boulevard Diderot and came to one those 'étoiles' where tourists are known to get totally confused and lost. On the North side of the Boulevard Voltaire, was a large tent where a farmer's market was taking place so they decided to have a buffet style luncheon. Josh dismissed the taxi and they stood on the sidewalk, in this mid-afternoon misty September day, taking in the sights.

Walking to the market, they saw that Parisians had already bought most of the produce, cheeses and meats from the vendors, many of whom were now preparing to close up shop.

Browsing from one stall to another, unable to decide on which cheese or pate to buy, the couple suddenly realized the mist had turned to rain and eating outside had become impractical.

They ran and ducked into the first café they saw, ordered cafés au lait with croissants as well as some delightful fruit pastries.

"Do you know where Père Lachaise is from here?" Jackie asked absentmindedly. "That way, I think, Josh said pointing to a vague North Easterly direction. Feel like walking in the rain?"

"Not yet, let's ride the worst of the shower off here and see what happens." Her boldness at making such a decision surprised her. Given his age, looks and standing, she technically should be grateful just to be here. But the roller coaster was high and so was she. She wanted this dreamlike adventure to last just a little while longer and would cling to it as gently, but also as hard as she could.

The rain finally subsided and since there was no sign of the weather improving, they started walking towards the general direction of the cemetery. Signs soon appeared showing them to be on the right track. It was still damp and cold, but neither seemed to notice.

The impressive cemetery gates soon appeared and they paused for a moment. A map outlining the burial plots of the better known residents was available and the couple aimed directly for the famous or rather infamous Morrison grave.

Scanning the list of distinguished 'guests', Jackie found Oscar Wilde, Proust, Sarah Bernhart, Molière and, her most beloved French songstress, Edith Piaf. They were surrounded by larger than life monuments to the great departed as well as to the ordinary folks who were finally among the elite after, perhaps, a life of trying to break through the class barriers.

People whispered in those seemingly hallowed paths. Morrison's grave was one of the smaller, less conspicuous ones, save for the flowers recently deposited by fans, some of whom were still hovering around the site. "I can see why the authorities are worried about keeping this area safe from vandalism." Josh said while assessing the half dozen or so jeans-cladded Americans, some looking rather unsavory, who stood by and appeared to have taken up residence in the general vicinity.

Jackie pointed to an open crypt, with various fast food cartons and alcohol-related containers lying within. "I don't think they've totally succeeded." She was going to go into her -why can't our American kids respect others' properties and laws while traveling - speech, but realizing this was neither the time, place nor company to do this with, she relented.

It fascinated her that in close to a 24 hour period spent together, she had managed to keep her life to herself. She, who voiced opinions in the supermarket, she, who talked about her children whenever there was a living person around, had spoken only of ideas and had lived those hours in the present tense only. She liked that. She made a mental note to strive for staying in this mode for as long as she could.

The sky was once again getting grayer and, surrounded by angels, ballerinas and old men reclining on their laurels, Jackie and Josh decided to start walking back to a livelier civilization.

It was too early for dinner, but the pastry shops were inviting as were the cafés, some of which with patrons sitting under awnings in spite of the cool, damp Sunday afternoon.

The establishment they chose appeared to provide the best shelter. A bottle of wine on the table, close to each other for warmth and comfort, they started the courtship all over again.

Having spent some years as a single woman in a large city, Jackie knew that the magic only lasted a few hours, sometimes a weekend, rarely a week, so she decided to bask into this one and forget about the rest of the world. It was her birthday after all and, she had no plans for the rest of her life.

The rain was now firmly established and they opted for an early dinner of steak-frites. The second bottle of wine lasted well beyond the meal and the short time they had planned to stop. The somber tint of the day was deepening into a darker shade as the hours passed from afternoon to night.

Too lazy or scared to awaken from a perfect moment, the couple prolonged the instant by sipping their wine and watching Parisians walk by, umbrellas in hand or a raincoat tightly closed around the collar.

They hadn't exchanged a word for a while when, as if inspired, Josh got up, left money on the table and hailed a cab, all the while dragging Jackie with him.

"Where are we going?" She asked. "Somewhere we can celebrate your birthday in private." He simply replied. Content to just follow, she got into the taxi, and settled on the seemingly luxurious interior. 'Another Mercedes, she thought smiling, who would have known that only two days ago we were total strangers sharing a ride.' She moved her legs so they rested against his and relaxed, not caring where they were going or how they would get there... So much for her help with French.

The taxi stopped in front of his hotel. The lobby was quiet at this time of day and they had the elevator to themselves.

Exhilarated, but wet, they were back in his room, laughing like children, intoxicated both by the wine and the anticipation of another night.

Jackie was amazed on how she could so easily dismiss so many years of trying to do the right thing and dive into this not mindless, but certainly emotionless affair. She crashed on the bed, wondering how she found herself back in this room after consciously repeating to herself that she had to be back in her hotel tonight. "Well, she thought, any plans for tomorrow? No? So what's the problem?"

None that she could see. Josh had turned out to be far different from her first impression during their initial encounter at the airport. He was certainly less liberal than she was, but was open to listen to new ideas, although she sensed his opinions were formed and would never change. However, this was inconsequential since she never intended to see him again after this night.

One aspect of his personality set him apart from other men Jackie had known over the years. He sincerely believed that women had been missing out too long on the pleasures of sex and, as he pointed out to her with a smile, he had found that "women who enjoy it are more demanding than any men I've ever talked to."

Objectively speaking, Jackie could never have fallen in love with someone like him. For a fraction of a second, she did seriously wonder about his life back home, but dismissed the thought as pointless... Who cared?

In the back of her mind, she had also feared that, once again, she was validating her life by being wanted by a man, but suddenly realized that it wasn't so. What she was experiencing was totally selfish and she didn't care, in fact she knew she would never see him again. She hadn't felt so self-indulgent since her days in New York after her divorce from Tommy.

"I should have gone back to my hotel." She said languorously, wanting him to reassure her.

"And leave me alone on my last night in Paris? And be alone on the night of your birthday?" He retorted. She almost told him that this was her choice. She could have had someone with her if she had wanted to, but remembered that any answer may cause him to realize she may have been using him, and she just looked up and smiled.

Josh picked up the phone and unconsciously took his jacket off, untied his shirt and sat next to Jackie. He ordered a bottle of champagne and some pastries from room service, then requested a wake up call for seven.

"I have a breakfast meeting at the airport before I go back to Chicago."

Jackie, now more conscious of her situation, tried to imagine what this scene would have looked like to an objective observer: here's an attractive, relatively young man with an over the hill woman playing coy in a Paris hotel room.

She dismissed the thoughts and concentrated on watching his hands placing the telephone receive back on its cradle and eventually come to rest on her, absentmindedly caressing her.

The champagne came, the pastries were eaten and, before a second glass was poured, a repeat performance of the previous night led them into the a dreamless sleep and, eventually the rude awakening of the phone ringing as a final bell that tolled for what would never be again.

Not many words were spoken that morning, but, unconsciously, Jackie put on the silk shirt he had given her to wear yesterday, threw her own, now discarded clothes in a laundry bag together with a few trinkets they had picked up at the flee market on their trek to the valley of death.

Although he was on a tight schedule, Josh asked if she wanted him to accompany her back to her hotel in a cab but she refused in a tone that didn't leave room for discussion.

They barely hugged, said goodbye and she was off, not sure exactly if she could find her hotel in the mental fog from which her brain was now desperately attempting to exit.

##

Jackie's hotel was actually a lot closer than she remembered. The sun was out, clouds hanging on the horizon. She found her way to her room without attracting too much attention and was going to crash until lunch when she saw a large bouquet of flowers on the window-side table.

Although she didn't think it was his style, she immediately thought Josh had sent them and smiled. Ripping open the envelope, however, her heart sank as she read 'Happy Birthday to the only one I love' it was signed Peter.

"Why did he have to do this?" Jackie thought, abruptly brought back to reality. She had specifically said to let her have this time alone. The flowers were beautiful, but stood as a reminder of how badly she had behaved.

She then got angry, first at her husband for denying her the residual pleasure of the last two days, then at herself for allowing him to ruin this mellow sensation she had hoped would last at least through the day.

Jackie and Peter had played roles for so long, they didn't know how to get out of character.

"I would feel better if I had been served with divorce papers instead." She thought, knowing that then, her guilt would be rightfully fed and she could hate him for whatever reason felt right at the time.

Jackie lied down on the bed for a while, hesitating between anger, self-pity and the urge to go home.

She must have fallen asleep. When she looked at the clock, it was past one and the sun had completely disappeared behind a curtain of white puffy clouds.

She picked herself up, gave one quick glance at the flowers like a child torn between the joy of a beautiful thing and the unfairness of it all, jumped in the shower, dressed quickly, glad to be back in her own clean underwear and left.

Le Shoppe looked very much like it did on the day she arrived and the server smiled at her in recognition.

"Vin rouge et Croque Monsieur?" He asked a twinkle in his eyes.

"S'il vous plait et pommes frites." Jackie said, smiling back.

Why tamper with perfection. Maybe she could recapture the mood she was in only a few days ago. The fries would nicely complement this comfortable, self-destructive pattern she was finding herself falling into.

Two hours later, she was back on the path to discovering Paris. She decided to keep it mindless and find some department store where she could see what she was missing out on in America's heartland.

She went on to rummage through bookshops, museums and galleries where some of the paintings were signed by recognizable names and, surprisingly enough, reasonably priced. Her practical side restored, she bought a few watercolors painted by artists on the bank of the Seine and decided to make it an early night.

Thinking about the wine she had never got to drink and a possible encounter with her hippy friends, she walked back to the hotel, making some provisions of fruits and vegetables along the way to help her get through early dinner hunger pangs.

Sitting at one of the garden tables, she munched on the crudités, sipped her wine and was pleased to see Richard and Nancy walk into the courtyard, arms full of packages. They immediately spotted her and waved in recognition.

"Hi, Jackie." Richard said. Then realizing how incongruous they must have looked, their retro look now combined with fashionable designer shopping bags, he continued. "We're getting ready to leave tomorrow and I promised some friends to bring back some stuff we can't find back home," he said, waving the guilty parcels, his existentialist image now shattered.

"Have a seat, she replied and pointing to her bottle, I'll ask the concierge for two more glasses."

"Well, Nancy interjected, we'll just go upstairs, get rid of those and come back in a bit."

They both walked away, leaving Jackie with a feeling of rejection. She leaned back in her chair, looked at the flower bed, now in its most colorful state, and tried to imagine what her own pitiful attempt at gardening now looked like. Back home the peonies were multiplying themselves at an alarming rate and the perennial garden which she had painstakingly planted last year had turned into a weed patch, just as Peter had predicted.

She was quite hopeless as a gardener now but she remembered a time when, as a good mother and wife, she would dutifully plant flowers on Memorial Day each year so that the house would be filled with blooms from July until the first frost. How pathetic can you get, she thought, trying to recapture the numb feeling she used to carry around with her during those early years which she spent with two babies in tow, showing the world how fulfilled she was in this role.

Drinking wine and watching other guests walking in and out of the hotel, Jackie wondered when and if there was ever a time when she had been truly herself.

If being oneself was to act according to natural instincts and with responsibility only to oneself, her New York experience and the last two days were probably the closest thing to the real Jackie as anything ever was... And that, in itself was a little scary.

New York was at the peak of disco, free love and Jackie's original fitness craze. Moving there with two children and no visible means of support had been looked upon as irresponsible and thoughtless, but it had worked out.

She was ambitious and at a time where few women dared to challenge the glass ceiling, Jackie managed to rapidly force her way into the board room.

She soon had the girls in private school and could hire a nanny to make sure they got home safely.

Her lifetime membership at Jack Lalanne's on 55th, and a daily run along riverside drive succeeded in proving to herself that she was a woman to be reckoned with.

In a way, she had to thank Tommy for letting her share as he did, in his business, and teaching her everything he knew, most of which she now used to get ahead in the insurance world. Only, she couldn't have stayed with him. He was in a rut and she was blooming.

The New York high had lasted four years. Four years of freedom, four years of travels, promotions and, one day what had been so exciting originally turned to boredom and she found herself ready for a change. New York is where she had met Janice and where Tommy came every so often to see the girls and drink with the two women. Jackie often wondered if anything had ever happened between her ex-husband and her best friend, but she never asked and had dismissed the thought a long time ago.

##

Sitting by herself in the garden of the Hotel des Grandes Ecoles, she was reliving the thrilling climb which had been her life in the City. Her thoughts were wandering to the years that followed when Richard and Nancy returned, bringing their own glasses and a fresh bottle of Beaujolais.

"We didn't see you all weekend, Nancy started. Did you take a side trip to the country?"

Jackie knew her question was innocent enough but felt herself lost for words, thanking her stars again that blushing was not something she knew how to do. The couple exchanged a glance and embarrassingly changed the subject.

"Nancy likes to give personalities to the places she visits, Richard said, and for as many years as we've come to Paris, we've been unable to agree on the one word that would describe its essence. Maybe we need a fresher point of view. What do you think Jackie?"

Jackie took a sip a wine, considering the question that had been put to her. "I don't know. My opinion is probably worthless since I've only been here a few days, and I can't think of one word. It seems like the people are one with their city and that one would not survive without the other: a symbiotic type of relationship." She paused, still pondering the question. "Paris is a living entity which allows only a selected few to share in its life."

"Interesting, Nancy interjected, my word for it was sensual, but Richard keeps insisting that hedonistic is more in tune with reality."

"Yes, Richard emphatically pronounced, look at the perfect gardens, the whole city looks perfect, the people try to look perfect and they don't easily let strangers in."

"Well, you've been here more often than I have, Jackie interjected but I can agree with both of you: I have seen the picture perfect parks and gardens and those 'green machines' constantly sweeping up the litter on the main streets, but when you think of it, Nancy's views aren't so different. Sensuality is a form of hedonism, which, as I see it, makes the people and their city in close synchronization."

Jackie listened to herself and wondered how long it had been since she'd had such a pretentious conversation. Years at least, she surmised. This kind of discussion had also been much easier to take as well as far more enlightening after she had smoked a few joints, but she noticed her more than half empty bottle and refilled her glass.

She hated herself for the realistic part of her personality which always eventually made fun of the existentialist within.

After she exchanged a few other brilliant thoughts with the couple, she hid a yawn behind her wine glass and excused herself for the night, wishing them a safe trip back home and somehow sad that they would not be there tomorrow when she returned from her next excursion into the unknown.

##

Jackie decided to use the 12 pound dumbbells for today's upper body exercises. "Military alternates." Called the trainer. "Four, Three, Two, one. Deltoids, move those arms, four, three, two one. Biceps, eight. Overhead for twelve reps."

Her body ached and she wondered why she was alone in the gym and the weights seemed lighter than usual. She lifted her arms for French presses, found her body falling backwards, and then floating on top of her workout mat. She dropped the dumbbells and tried to reach for a solid handle to grip for safety.

Jackie woke up in a sweat and sat up wondering where she was and how she got there. After a few seconds, her heart stopped pounding as she realized it had just been a dream. The room was in total darkness and her automatic reflex was to look for security in her husband sleeping on the other half of the bed.

This is when she remembered she was in Paris and her previously safe world was light years away. She turned the bedside lamp on and tried to remember some of the calming breathing exercises she had learned over the last year, while preparing for this adventure.

None of them worked. The feeling of emptiness and void within her was bottomless. She wanted to get up, go to the washroom or read, but was glued in place by the dread that any movement would cause her to fall into the deepest abyss of depression.

As far as anxiety attacks go, this was the worst she ever experienced, at least since the girls had gotten over their rebellious teenage years. A litany of long forgotten prayers came to mind. She concentrated on remembering the words, deliberately bringing them forward in her mind, one line at the time.

Sitting with her head now leaning on the back board, she closed her eyes and started relaxing. She wished there was someone she could call or talk to, but what would she say? She couldn't even find anything to tell herself, how could she relate her feelings to someone else? The thought of dying right here and now seemed appealing, but she knew it wouldn't happen and she'd have to, once again, get over this hopelessness that had been creeping over her for the last few years and was now reaching new lows. The roller coaster had reached the top of the hill. The steep drop had started.

She suddenly remembered the blank journal Josh had purchased for her at the flea market on Sunday, saying she should record this weekend for posterity. She had laughed then, but now the need to communicate was strong and the journal her only outlet.

"Where do I start?" Jackie wrote. She sat, staring at the blank page for what seemed like an hour, wondering how to even attempt to describe her state of mind.

"It's three in the morning here, which means it's either seven or eight at night at home. I'm losing my grip on the reality of home. Who would have thought I'd miss it. But I don't really. Am I scared? Is this what my whole life has been for?"

Realizing her lack of logic or cohesive thinking, she put down the pen and decided to find sleep again, this time getting up to open the drapes before turning the light off so she would readily recognize her surroundings next time she opened her eyes.

It was past eight when she woke up, glad that the last part of the night had been dreamless.

Still disturbed by the night's dream, Jackie decided that a return to some routine may help. She put on running shorts and shoes and left for a morning trot. Fall was definitely in the air and Jackie shivered.

She was barely out the portal door when she realized that unless she found a park rather quickly, she would be tripping over innocent pedestrians who only wanted to get to work, school or even breakfast. She ended up in some botanical garden, only to be told that running was not allowed as it disrupted the harmony of the site.

Feeling dejected, she slowly found her way back to the hotel, knowing that she could run along the Seine, but the moment had passed. She climbed the stairs to her room and stared outside the window at the garden, looking for some answer.

What am I doing here? She thought. She sat at the small desk, her eyes avoiding the flowers which accusingly remained alive; her fingers reached for a pen, she tore a page out of the diary and started writing.

"Dear Janice," she paused and wondered if she had anything at all to say. "I know I said I wouldn't write or call, but I'm sitting here in my hotel room, trying to figure out what I'm doing here and you're the only one who can relate to me when I'm in this frame of mind.

I met a man when I got here and, well, just remember the way we were back in our New York days and you'll pretty much know what happened. I needed this so bad, but at the same time, I'm sure this isn't what I came here for.

Why is it that every time I have something memorable to tell it has to do with a man? Am I so dependent on what the males of the specie think of me that I can only function under those circumstances? But then, successful men surround themselves with young attractive women, don't they? And they don't get accused of being female dependent.

I'm so confused. I thought for sure I'd see why I had come here quickly, deal with it and go on. I think I had convinced myself that someone or something would come and show me the way... So to speak. As it is, I'm just sitting here wondering where the hell to go from here. There's been no sign, nothing to get me going in the right mental direction; the question is, however, will I know the signs when I see them? OK, I guess this weekend didn't help, but I confess that it brought back some awesome memories I never thought I could recapture.

Even as I write, I am tempted to go into the typical post card stuff about weather and tourist attractions. I can't seem to be able to peel my outer shell and find out who's actually inside... Assuming there is more to me than meet the eye! Maybe I am that shallow?

I'm not only at a stalemate about my future; I'm starting to question my past. Did I make the right decisions, what if... But then I know that what ifs only lead to sentences such as 'what if I had wheels, I may be a bicycle.' So I'll spare us both.

I don't see any future, except for a long series of boring attempt at having a life until it finally becomes politically correct to give up and rot. Cheery isn't it?

I was just going to ask about your family, but to be honest, I don't much care. At this point, I don't even care about mine. I'm sort of numb, but functioning well with the occasional anxiety attack. Doesn't make for a novel does it?"

She stopped writing and smiled, remembering this goal she had as a girl to write 'the greatest novel of all times by a woman author.' Something else she would never do. Her smile faded and she reached for the paper, ready to tear up the letter, but forced herself to continue.

"You know, Janice, I always wonder what would have happened if I had stayed in New York, instead of moving on... Would I be CEO of a large company? Actually, I would probably be dead or insane by now. We did some pretty crazy things then. The kids kept me sane."

Jackie put the pen down, remembering one more of her failures.

One day, Jackie told her friend of an opportunity to move to Bermuda to work for an International firm; Janice voiced some doubts about it, but Jackie hesitated only long enough to convince her then prepubescent girls that it would be great. "It'll give you a great place to visit in the winter." Jackie had told her best friend to bring her to her side.

Memories of Tommy's and her first encounter with the islands were still vivid and she moved ahead with blinders, her eyes covered with rose-colored glasses.

She soon found that living on the islands was far different from visiting as a tourist. As a woman in a country with a fifties' style culture where greed is the main capital, she found herself working in a cubicle with other professionals. Regardless of abilities, islands natives and women often didn't rate an office, or she later found out, the salaries only white male expatriates seemed to be entitled to. Many of those were dead wood executives sent to Bermuda as a reward for years of service and consequently lacking in the efficiency and up-to-date knowledge department.

Jackie had tried to make it work but her sense of fairness was on alert and, the way she saw how exploited she and some of her women colleagues were, she knew that this island relationship wouldn't last well beyond the first year.

The kids were getting restless and complained about the mandatory school uniforms, the lack of malls and mostly about the fact that visiting their friends was almost out of the question. They hated the bus, Jackie would not let them ride their bikes on the narrow winding roads and they were too young to drive a scooter. So, in addition to the pressure and sometime humiliation she had to endure in the workplace, she also had to suffer her children's whining at home every night. Then there were the nanny's escapades to the nearby pub where hotel staff, imported from the less fortunate areas of the world to toil 15 hours a day, hung out and drank.

Her career, far from being helped by this move, was alienating some of her former contacts and she didn't know where to turn to find work again back home. She was no longer invited to national conferences, and soon recognized that her dreams of European escapades were turning into being asked to serve coffee when an important guest visited from the home office in England.

With her self-esteem at its lowest and the fear of losing her lifestyle, she was happiest when walking into town, an obvious resident, and having tourist think she must me quite important to be able to work in this paradise-like setting. Running in the early morning hours on the railroad trail where she had a shot of aromatherapy and a sense of peace was also helping her cope with this secluded life.

She didn't date often since most singles' idea of fun was to drink themselves into oblivion and sleeping around with anything that moved, something she was not interested in at the time.

That's how Peter found her. He was attending a conference on technology at the hotel where Jackie sometimes hung around at tea time, mostly to meet tourists from home and play up her local residence.

He was about her age, handsome, but reserved, and if she hadn't been so desperate for conversation, this version of history would never have been.

They played tennis; she took him for a tour of the country on her scooter. They toasted their homeland with rum swizzles until the early hours of the morning, exchanged business cards, and retreated to their separate lairs.

Peter hadn't even made a pass, let alone a great impression, so when he wrote to say that he was planning a vacation back to the Islands over the summer, one based on her availability, she was tempted to ignore the letter or write a curt note back making some excuse why he shouldn't visit.

The kids, however, convinced her that perhaps he had business ties which could be helpful to her, and, their ultimate goal, allow them to return home. She relented and wrote a brief, non committal memo-style note, to say she would be pleased to see him again in July.

She didn't go to the airport, first because she wasn't about to take the bus, and then she didn't want to look too interested.

His call came in mid-afternoon. He was staying in a nearby hotel and invited her to dinner that night. The relaxed atmosphere, the wine and long walk along the rocky shore eventually brought them one step closer to what eventually resulted in a proposal, and the offer of a new life in Wisconsin where his technology business was prospering beyond expectation. There would be room for her to work there or so he told her.

The kids were ecstatic. Milwaukee wasn't New York, but it meant going back to wearing clothes that didn't smell like mildew and experiencing the cool scent of the first snow just before the skating season began. And you can drive from there. They would have a car again.

It was late November, a windy, wet one, only like you'll find in the Midwest, when they landed at Mitchell International after a brief stop in Atlanta, and proceeded to build a new life. The new house, the renovations, the decorators together with the humiliating rejections Jackie received from potential employers resulted in her sedately settling in her new environment and searching for new recipes to keep the family happy.

Jackie picked up the pen, now making a flame-like figure on the back of her used up boarding pass. That was it. No more to say.

"Anyway, I better go. I'm not even sure what I'll do next. Hope the City is treating you well!

Love,

Jackie"

By that time, the sky was gray again. Jackie just stretched out on the bed, staring at the ceiling, waiting for something to happen.

It was well past noon when she woke up still in her running clothes. She hopped in the shower and decided this was going to be a day of local wondering.

She walked out of the hotel, found a bistro where she ordered a baguette with pate de campagne and a beer. Jackie didn't really wish to drink, but coffee and sodas were too expensive. She then walked around exploring small art galleries and shops before walking back to her hotel and finally spending a dreamless night of total rest.

Jackie woke up at seven as she did at home, her body now completely tuned-in to the time zone. The day was again wet and gray but she was ready to take on the world, once again. The roller coaster was crawling back up.

She crossed to the right bank on the Pont Neuf and walked all morning towards Sacré-Coeur. She made a point to lunch at the well known Mère Catherine where she drank her first wine of the day.

She lingered there for a while. Space warmers were lit up so the patrons could still eat outside under the canopy in relative comfort in spite of the cool and damp weather. By two thirty, she was ready to go and explore that part of the city.

Montmartre was alive with tourists mixed with prostitutes, drug dealers and your average slackers. Jackie picked a sleazy-looking outdoor bar and ordered wine. Sitting outside, halfway through the day's second bottle of Beaujolais, she finally determined that wine was the only cure for the sudden panic attacks that were sure to come back and haunt her. She was willing to do anything to numb the nameless pain that was relentlessly growing in the pit of her stomach. Nothing so far, no sign of what she was supposed to do or feel. A deep sense of emptiness mixed with guilt is what she was experiencing, and those feelings appeared to lessen after each sip of wine.

The gloomy curtain of thoughts lifted after the third glass. Jackie then spotted another patron, sitting two tables away and sporting a leather jacket with an American flag on the sleeve. A surge of patriotism or perhaps just the thought of speaking to someone from home, led her to stare, and then smile at the stranger when he finally acknowledged her presence.

"Hi, she started. You American?"

"Yeah." he replied with a 'What's it to you' attitude and quickly glanced away. "I am too, Jackie insisted. Where are you from?" Realizing he was dealing with one of those nosy women who wouldn't leave him alone until he volunteered some information, he relented. "Boston, but I'm here now." he said as abruptly as he could without being totally rude and turned to look at the street where cars, cabs and scooters were fighting for their place in continuous traffic.

This was more than Jackie expected and she conceived a plan to befriend him so she could discover this part of the city, not only with someone who probably knew it, but without having to wear her brains out trying to speak French. She turned her chair to face his.

"I'm from the mid-west, Chicago area." She said, thinking there was no way she'd admit she was from Milwaukee. Over the years, she'd often said she lived in Wisconsin, but never could she bring herself to concede to Milwaukee. She knew this was snobby, but didn't care.

He still didn't seem overly interested, but she had no intention of letting go. The wine had finally found its way to her brain and she was determined.

Assessing the situation, she estimated the man to be in his early to mid thirties. Dark curly hair circled his face, reminding her of the afro perms some of her friends had in simpler times. His curls were the real thing, however. His complexion was dark, the tuff on the hands holding the beer matching the head and a five o'clock shadow already shading his cheeks.

"You been in Paris long, she asked?" Answering as though to pacify an annoying child, he took a sip from his drink and shrugged; "a couple of months, I guess."

Jackie realized he had no interest in the conversation and looked for something that would trigger his interest. She tried to read the label on his T-shirt, or see what magazine he was carrying, but could only determine that it wasn't anything she was familiar with.

About to give up, she picked up her glass, only to have an obviously drunken passerby come too close, causing her to jerk her elbow and spill the wine. The guilty man bent over her table: "Désolé, Mademoiselle, he slurred, mais tout de même, vous chargez combien aujourd'hui?" Between the heavy 'Provencal' accent and the slur, she had no idea what the man wanted.

"Pardon, je ne comprends pas." She replied in the best French she could muster, all the while trying to blot the red wine from her pants.

"Eh bien, mais t'es une pute, non?" the man insisted. "C'est combien?"

Jackie was becoming quite flustered and uncomfortable. Trying to remain cool, she noticed a few people smiling at her demise and adopted her sternest look to tell the man to leave her alone.

His response was to sit across from her and put his hand on her knee. The man was wearing a plaid shirt and a slept-in looking pair of brown work pants. His breath smelled of beer and garlic and he sniffled between each words. Disgusting, Jackie thought.

"Garçon." She called, hoping one of the staff would take notice and come to her aid. The young American was now staring; a twinkle in his eyes betrayed some amusement, one she did not share at this particular moment.

He then slowly rose from his chair, grabbed the man by the arm and gently but firmly pushed him away from the table, back into the pedestrian traffic. "Madame n'est pas interessée."

Embarrassed, but genuinely grateful, Jackie raised her eyes ready to thank him, but he seemed so amused at the whole situation that she couldn't help laughing herself.

"This isn't a place for someone like you, he said. You should stick to the trendier tourist areas so no one thinks you're a prostitute."

"Is this what it was?" she asked, half insulted by his assuming she was a typical tourist, half pleased that someone could mistakenly think she could still charge for her fifty year old body, however drunk the man was. "I really couldn't understand a word he was saying. Let me buy you a drink."

She found out his name was David and he had temporarily given up a successful career in finance after a messy divorce. He had quit his job to avoid alimony and his share of marital property was being squandered on the streets of Paris. Jackie somehow managed to have him tell his life story without telling about her own story and found herself enjoying the conversation.

The wine was gone and he seemed anxious to leave. Jackie asked for his phone number and suggested she returned the next day. She had no intention to repeat the Josh experiment, but she felt this man could show her parts of the city only known to Parisians and she was interested.

This time she took the Métro back to the left bank, picked up some inexpensive wine and walked back to her hotel .

Now that Jackie was in her room, the flowers still fresh on the table, reality was trying to creep back into her life. She lied down on the bed, hands joined behind her head, wondering what to do next. Nothing was happening; no doors were opening or closing. The wine high was wearing off and a pang of fear rose up in her stomach. She thought of calling home, but then envisioned life back in the suburb and settled back on the pillow.

She mentally calculated what she owed on her room and how many days she had left to subsist on the money she had. Her heart started beating faster and she rose to open the bottle of wine. She passed out, an hour later, having no clue what time it was or what she was going to do next.

##

Jackie woke up after nine, surprised to see the sun shining behind the curtains. She lifted her head and a headache mixed with dizziness caused her to sink back into bed. She now realized her last meal was lunch the day before and dinner has passed her by between the liters of wine.

She could feel her brain expanding and applying pressure to her aching skull. Her body was throbbing as if it had a million bed springs attached to its nervous system. She looked at the night table and saw the glass of water she had place there, an old habit from home, painfully reached for her bag, dug up two aspirins and sank back to sleep.

It was after three when she woke again. Still in pain, Jackie crawled into the shower and got dressed in the same clothes she had on the day before. She then crossed the street and bought a baguette, some cheese and pate with the most inexpensive wine the shop had to offer.

Back in her room, hair still wet from the shower and disheveled, she sat at the table, staring at the flowers and ate as much of the bread and food as she could, washing it all down with wine to drown the headache. She eventually crawled back into bed without even turning the lights on this dark late afternoon fall day; her clothes still on, she fell asleep again.

##

Jackie was in her mother's house. It wasn't exactly the house she remembered, but in her mind this was her mom's house. It was dark and a few people seem to be fighting about something. She couldn't recognize most of them, but the feeling that she should stop the fight was strong. Her mother was sitting on an old couch, looking sad and so small.

Jackie didn't remember ever knowing her mom looking so thin. She seemed like she was wasting away and her eyes cried for attention. Jackie bent down towards her and gave her a slight hug saying that everything would be alright. Her mom looked up at her and just shook her head.

Jackie suddenly had this urge to just let her mom be and leave. The disapproval she had seen in her sad eyes reminded her of how she could never please her and it was just better to go. There was no winning for her here. The quarrel was still going on around her, but she raced down the stairs.

She suddenly stopped running and had the strong feeling this was the last time she would see her mother alive. A wave rushed through her body and she ran back, climbed the steps two at a time and rang the bell. Her mom opened the door and Jackie just put her arms out held her tighter than she ever had before, feeling love she didn't know she had for the woman who had raised her.

Jackie's family had never been one to demonstrate affection and once she had decided to take the lead, her mother had suffered a shoulder injury and any kind of contact provoked agonizing pain.

This night, in this dream, was in fact the first time she had held her mother in her arms. It felt good. It felt right. Still holding her mother, she closed her eyes tight to etch this moment in her memory forever.

Jackie woke up crying. She couldn't stop. Her sobs were so loud, she became concerned that someone would hear and buried her head in the pillow. She only fell back to sleep when all her energy had been spent and her conscious mind could no longer cope with the mixture of joy experienced in this dream and the pain that surfaced when she woke.

She woke up at six and just lay on the bed, staring at the ceiling until her chest tightened up, remembering that she couldn't afford staying in this hotel another night and her reservation was up.

##

Jackie got up, looked at herself in the mirror and thought she saw a ghost: she was pale, her hair spiking with a few gray strands on the temple, her eyes now sporting bags under them.

She shrugged, tried to brush some sense onto her head and decided to check and see how much her hotel would take from her fast dwindling money. She considered using the credit card, but something inside kept her from giving in to the temptation. She still had an open return ticket; she would just go home when she ran out.

She shivered as soon as she opened the door. Fall had finally settled in and the air was cool and crisp. She crossed the courtyard, deserted at this time of morning, and entered the other wing of the hotel where the reception area was.

The bill was higher than she had calculated. The various taxes that applied, her first breakfast, all added up to more than she had left. Taken aback, trying to keep her composure, she gave in and handed a credit card. She knew this was wrong. She had been unfaithful, she hadn't even called home or said thank you for the flowers, this was wrong. She'd make it up sometime, she thought.

Back in the room, she started packing, throwing her toiletries and clothes, most of which should have been washed or cleaned, in her backpack and saving a clean change of clothes in her travel bag. She had no clue where she would go. Not home was the only thing she knew for sure.

It was close to eleven when she emerged from her room and walked out the coach door without any idea of what would come next.

At the corner, she saw her favorite café and decided to stop, one last time, for lunch.

The same waiter was there as had been on this first day when she had just landed in Paris. He smiled and she ordered her usual croque-monsieur and frites with a bottle of wine. It wasn't a mistake this time, she wanted a whole bottle.

For some reason, the circle, the fountain, the scooters, the people, none of them looked as they had only a week ago. What she saw now was a neighborhood where dramas were being played between these men and women whose night had probably been filled with smoke, wine, loneliness or love.

The first glass of wine went down like a cozy blanket on a winter day. The sun was warming the pavement and her mind was enjoying its slow alcohol induced numbing.

It was three by the time she picked up her bags and headed for the metro. Back to Sacré-Coeur where she had read was the least expensive lodging you could find; but first, back to the bar where she had met David.

She walked along the street unsure which bar was the one she had been to. Then she saw him. He was wearing the same jacket and looked as though he hadn't moved since she had last seen him. She smiled and sat at his table.

He barely acknowledged her. "I had to move out of my hotel." She simply stated. His eyes were glassy and had a strange reflection to them. "Leaving the city?" he inquired. "No," Jackie answered "I just can't stay on the left bank. I'm running out of money."

The waiter came by and she ordered a bottle of wine, motioning him to bring her table mate another of whatever he was drinking. David just glanced at her and stared back at the traffic and accepted the drink with a quick nod.

Jackie waited until the wine had worked its magic again before interrupting his silence. "I was hoping to find you here. I thought you may know of a cheap hotel I could crash in."

He looked at her again, and, she suddenly realized he had forgotten who she was and why she was talking to him. She thought it best to let it be. He was obviously high on something and his memory may return once he was back in control. Jackie drifted back in time when being high was what people did.

##

Chase Manhattan plaza, circa 1978. You could get stoned at lunchtime, just breathing the second hand Marijuana smoke emanating from all the financial executives who couldn't face an afternoon sober or straight.

Singles' parties usually took place on weekdays since everyone had weekend plans: Fire Island, Atlantic City, Boston; or family obligations: kids to pick up from an ex, sick parent in Connecticut, spouses who had no clue their better halves were not working late but picking up female colleagues or girlfriends in the city.

Drinking alcohol on weeknights was out of the questions since most participants could not afford being hung over the next morning. Marijuana was therefore the drug of choice, sometimes baked in brownies for those who were unable to inhale the smoking kind. A few of Jackie's friends had graduated to Coke, but she hadn't; she refused to relinquished control and after experimenting with various substances, she had made up her mind that the only acceptable one was the common weed.

She was brought back to reality when she felt David staring at her. She could tell he was searching his memory in an attempt to remember who she was. He then suddenly threw his head back and laughed: "Hey, now I know. You're the one who was accosted by the drunk the other day. The prostitute." And he laughed even louder.

"Well," Jackie answered "I'm not a prostitute." She felt uncomfortable. "Remember, you saved me from that jerk?" He looked at her more closely. "Yeah, I remember." He paused. "What's up?" he asked, having totally forgotten the earlier comments.

Jackie wondered if talking to this man was of any use, but she had nothing else to do. "I checked out of the hotel. I'm running out of money and I wondered if you knew of a really cheap place where I could stay." This time, he stared at her for a while.

"I know someone who told me his girlfriend was looking for a roommate. How long are you here for?"

Jackie wished she knew. "I don't know. A few days, a week, who knows?" He considered this. "Well I could ask her. She told him she couldn't pay for the phone this month so she may just charge you for that."

Jackie wasn't sure about that. A cheap hotel was one thing, a roommate another. She could save a lot of money, but she didn't' even know the girl. She hadn't responded to David's suggestion, but realized he had reached for his cell phone and was already talking to his friend. I was only a minute before he hung up and turned to her.

"Well," he said, "I can take you there anytime. Patrice told me she's home right now. What do you think?"

Jackie was taken aback. Her wine was low and she had no place to go. "OK." She replied wondering what she was getting herself into, but not really caring.

She paid and followed David through a number of small streets lined with traditional six story houses. She wondered if she could retrace her steps, but it didn't seem to matter at this point.

The house they stopped at was one of these former 'hotels particuliers' converted into apartments or rooming houses. The concierge was cleaning the sidewalk; he waved at David and let the couple into the building. The smells were of garlic and boiled vegetables, mixed with cheap perfume and cigarette smoke. They walked up four sets of stairs and stopped in front of the first door, marred by the many fists that had undoubtedly pounded on it over the last century.

A young woman answered the door. She had very dark, obviously dyed hair, long dangling earrings, a low cut black clinging sweater and a micro mini black skirt. The only color was that of her strikingly green eyes. She acknowledged David with a kiss on both cheeks and looked at Jackie, wondering what she was doing there.

"Patrice told me you were looking for someone to pay your phone bill. I ran into this woman who is looking for cheap place to crash for a few days or whatever. What do you think?"

He checked himself, having forgotten the obvious.

"Denise, this is," he hesitated for a moment. "Jackie" Jackie said, shaking the other woman's hand and realizing David still didn't remember who she was.

They walked into the apartment, Denise and David continuing the conversation in French. The living-dining room was one and the same and the two bedrooms were smaller than many walk-in closets; all opened onto a hallway which ended with a tiny kitchen with a minuscule refrigerator and a microwave oven.

The bedroom she would be sleeping in was filled with discarded bags, decrepit furniture and a bed that was little more than a cot with an antique quilt which was almost invisible under the pile of clothes covering it. "I'll clear that out." Denise said grabbing the bundle with both hands and running to next room to dump it on her own bed.

"It's not the Ritz," said David, "but it's cheap."

Jackie was in a daze. She had never seen anything quite like this. She dumped her bags on the bed, thanked him and handed Denise the equivalent of fifty dollars for the few days she would spend in the apartment. She wondered what would happen next.

Denise and David left her standing there and she heard them mutter something about finding a beer in the refrigerator.

Jackie looked around. She didn't take her clothes out of the bags. She just thought she would use whatever was absolutely necessary to live here for a few days. She hid most of her money in the travel bag, only keeping enough for a few days in her wallet.

"They must be talking about how this old lady had ended up on this doorstep." She thought to herself.

Coming out a few minutes later, she saw that they were now sitting at the kitchen table drinking and, from what she understood, talking about their plans for the evening.

They both turned, looking as if they wondered how she got there. Denise shrugged and the conversation continued all in French.

Jackie had tried to think of a good story to tell about where she was from and how she got here, but she soon realized this was a place where no one cared who you were and where conversations were more about getting high and where the next party was, then other people's lives.

"Hey, Jackie, I don't have an extra key." Denise said. "What time do you plan on being here tonight?"

Jackie had no idea what she was going to do or where she would go, so she shrugged and remained silent. "Maybe she'd like to come with us to the club." David said. It was Denise's turn to shrug. "Moi, j'veux bien." She said.

The three of them left and started back towards Montmartre. Jackie remained silent. She would just pretend to be a fly on the wall and remain invisible. The wine had lost its effect and she was getting hungry.

The trio finally entered a bar, one with painted windows and smoke oozing out of the stainless steel trimmed wooden door. At first, Jackie was blinded. The bar was dark and the crowd sitting on the stools cast shadows that appeared to be moving in slow motion. Some turned and greeted the newcomers' entrance. Jackie was introduced and left to stand and stare at the characters represented in this bar.

Before she could decide on whether to stay or find some excuse to leave, someone put a glass of wine in her hands. "Pour Madame." This youngish longhaired man uttered in her ear.

"Oh, merci." She took a sip and tried to concentrate on what he was saying, talking at the speed of light, all in French.

Oblivious to the fact that she didn't understand his diatribe, he offered his hand and introduced himself as Jean-François. She took the hand, nodded and only said "Jackie".

He was quite tall for a Frenchman. His hair was light in color and limp across his shoulder; his eyes were of an indefinite color and shinning in spite of the dim light. His hands were moving as fast as his lips and torrents of words came out at once.

She drank quickly and found another glass in her hand as soon as the first was empty. Jean-Francois lit a joint and offered it to her. Jackie hadn't smoked-up in years, but this seemed to be like a good time and place to start again. She took a deep drag off the cigarette but years of healthy smoke-free living caused her to choke. With the crowd now concentrating on her coughing, tears flowing out of her eyes, humiliation set in.

When she finally regained some composure, everybody laughed and returned to their previous conversation. "Je suis desolée." She apologized to her new-found companion who just stood there, smiling, oblivious to her feelings.

"Je vois que çà n'est pas pour vous." He said, realizing, even in his daze, that Jackie could not stand the smoke, dug in his jacket pocket to find some substitute substance she could have with no chocking effect. He found what he was looking for and just threw it in her wine.

Jackie had put her glass down while getting her breath and she now turned towards the bar, reaching for it, attempting to rid her throat of that dry, uncomfortable feeling brought on by the smoke. As soon as she took the first two gulps, she realized there was something strange happening to her.

The floor seemed higher than it was before and the ceiling lower. The conversations came as separate syllables, none of which she could understand. She reached out for support and found Jean-Francois' shoulder. He accommodated her and helped her to a stool which had just become vacant. She rested her head in her hands and didn't even attempt to talk.

Everyone now seemed to be laughing at her and she heard noises as if a football team was playing just outside the door.

She felt hands on her waist and while what was left of her thoughts wished them away, her body would not respond. Another glass of wine was put in front of her but it seemed too far away to grasp.

How long she was in this state, she didn't know. Time had passed. Her new companion had helped himself to her lips and was nibbling at her neck, all the while holding her steadily with one arm while the other roamed over her body.

It wasn't a bad sensation; she knew she was losing control and, in her stupor, could not decide whether she cared or not.

David and Denise finally came over and announced their group was going back to the apartment. Jean-François was invited as well. She got up from the stool, found her jacket on the floor and almost fell trying to recover it. She followed the group outside. The cool fresh air had a sobering effect, but she was still confused and weak.

It was close to two in the morning and the sidewalks were teeming with life, many representing sub-cultures that only roamed the streets of Monmartre after hours. Jackie floated back to the apartment, Jean-François guiding her through the human obstacles.

Once there, David, Denise, her boyfriend and a few tag-along's crashed in the living room, and danced to some soft jazz tunes on the radio. Jackie followed their cue, weaving around to the mellow sounds. Jean-Francois swiftly led her towards her room while unzipping her pants and helping her out of her sweater.

As soon as she felt cool air on her skin, Jackie pushed him away and as clearly as she could, announced that she was going to sleep and, no, he couldn't come along. The young man was as wasted as she was and his strength had only come from her weakness. He just shrugged and went back to the living room to crash with the others.

Jackie woke up with the worst headache she had ever had. She couldn't remember most of the previous night but was glad she was alone and, from what she could tell, that she had been alone all night.

She had to get out of this apartment before anyone else woke up. She didn't have a key to come back but she didn't care. She could probably find David somewhere at a café later.

She quickly put on her jeans and turtle neck and noticed as she picked up her jacket that it was now stained with cigarette burns. She walked out of her room and found her way through the few bodies asleep on the living room floor, none of which stirred as she opened the door and left.

She started walking aimlessly and soon found herself in front of Sacré-Coeur. Climbing the steps was hard; she was breathing laboriously when she reached the church. Ignoring the tourists and souvenir shops and entered the sanctuary. She still has no feeling of God's presence but nonetheless found a pew and kneeled, holding her head in her hands.

There had been no signs. There had been no doors opening or new opportunities for finding a better self. "If this was a contest," Jackie thought, "I have lost." All she had found was more despair and nothing to give her hope for another half century of life. She now understood that her youth had been lived in a very special time and being young again, in this new century, was not something she wanted to be.

Jackie prayed. No one answered.

She left the church, forced herself to eat something at a corner pastry shop and continued walking, in spite of the headache and now nausea that occasionally shook her body. She had lost all sense of time and day.

It must have been late afternoon when she found herself in front of Denise's apartment. She still had her luggage there but didn't think she would be staying the week. She waived to the concierge who let her in without questions. The door to the apartment was ajar, so she pushed it open and found the same bodies, still on the living room, now awake and staring at her. "Bonjour" she said trying to lighten up the mood.

No one responded. David got up and motioned her over to the kitchen. She walked behind him, noticing that her bedroom door was open, certain she had closed it earlier.

"It's Jean-François" he said. Jackie stared at him, not understanding what this was about. "He went to your room, I guess after you left this morning. They're saying that he was so upset about your leaving that he shot some bad dope and when Denise got up, she noticed the door opened and saw him lying unconscious on your bed."

She was speechless. What did she have to do with this? "I think," David continued, "that you better gather your stuff and leave."

"Is Jean-François OK?" Jackie asks. "We don't know yet, but it doesn't look good. It's always worse for people who are HIV positive. They need special medical attention."

"HIV?" Jackie screamed. "I could have slept with him and it's my fault that he OD'd?"

"Just go." David pushed her towards her room, watched her pick up her backpack. "Where is my travel bag?" she asked. "I don't think you had one," he replied. "But I had my extra money and all the clean clothes I had left in it."

Tears were coming up but she didn't want him to have the satisfaction. Had she ever been the sucker. David just turned around keeping the door open for her to leave. She looked all around the room, glanced in the other rooms, saw no sign of her bag and left.

It was dark out. She had nowhere to go.

Ironically, her now shabby jacket and dirty backpack gave her a sense of belonging. She was as much of a loser as those kids. More so. She should have known better. She remembered a time when anger turned into action and problem solving. Not today.

She walked aimlessly and, exhausted, sat at a small corner table in a café somewhere in Paris. She ordered whatever the board announced as a special and a carafe of wine. Bringing the alcohol level in her blood helped but didn't give her any idea as to what to do next. She suddenly panicked: her passport may be missing. She opened her backpack, rummage through dirty clothes which scattered on the sidewalk around her table. Then she felt the glossy cardboard cover and had a sigh of relief. This feeling didn't last when she found the open plane ticket missing. She had put it with her extra cash. Jackie wanted to leave everything there and walk off, but she did pick up her now dusty clothes and closed her bag.

She wasn't going home. Not just yet. Not the way she looked. She spent as much time at the café as she could, numbing her pain with wine, nurturing her depression with thoughts of just hanging here until someone declared her dead.

It must have been after midnight when she left the café and started walking again aimlessly. No one approached her. She was just one of those night shadows no one really notices. She passed a restaurant with an outdoor terrace and heard English spoken. She almost stopped and approached the dinners, but, from the look in their eyes when they saw her, she turned her head and walked on.

That was it. She didn't want to hear French anymore. She wanted to be able to speak without feeling inadequate or strange. He brain couldn't handle any more information or conflict.

Jackie sat on a park bench, somewhere in Paris. There were still some late strollers around the park, but they paid no attention to her. She hoped no one would notice that she was falling asleep in spite of the cold, humid Paris night.

##

She woke up with a start when she felt something tugging at her feet. Her heart was pounding, trying to figure out where the rest of the body was. It was still dark but Jackie remembered where she was and saw a stray dog trying to get comfortable near her. Tears welled in her eyes as she wished she could be that animal and snuggle up to someone warm.

Gathering her backpack which had served as a pillow, she got up and started walking again. Light was crawling up in the east and, Jackie tried to assess where she was. She found some change and entered a public restroom on the curb of a large avenue. As soon as she went in, she saw this old woman, dirty, circle under her eyes, staring at her. That was her own reflection. This is what she had become. Was this who she was? Was she finally in touch with her 'real' self?

She splashed water on her face, tried to comb her hair, but only succeeded in accentuating the look of despair in the women facing her.

Walking out, Jackie glanced at the city map on the latrine wall and saw that she was still in the same area, having walked in circles the previous night. She saw that the train station was close by and decidedly aimed for that building.

The mood was still subdued at this early time of the morning but lines were already forming around the Eurostar ticket counter. She looked in her wallet to see if she had enough money, came across the credit card and, in a moment of clarity bent it, ripped it apart and threw it in the waste basket sitting by the rope which kept the line in order.

There was enough. She bought a ticket to London, went to the platform and was glad to see the train was already there, waiting to leave in an hour. Finding a seat facing forward, she crashed and, again fell asleep, this time hugging her bag as if someone was threatening to take it.

London. Somehow Jackie thought that this time maybe this city would give her some answers. The sun was out when the train emerged from the tunnel and she woke up, thinking she was back in the plane, almost two weeks ago, and that the last few days had only been a nightmare. Reality set back in as she watched the villages and suburbs go by with their century old homes adjoining the more modern townhouses.

The train station was buzzing with activity and surrounded by taxis, busses and humanity which seemed to go in every direction.

The sun had been replaced by large, ominous gray cotton puffs, ready to burst. She followed a crowd around the building and walked aimlessly to where she believed was the Thames. She came across homeless teenagers, sitting in doorways with their dogs and smoking their first cigarette of the day. A woman, looking about her age was meandering around with a bag filled with remnants of food and garbage.

Jackie couldn't stop. Now that she could understand conversations and comments, she didn't know how to handle it and didn't care. She kept walking without the feeling she could ever stop. That bench was too dirty, this one wet with the drizzle that had started after she left the station. This restaurant was too fancy considering how she looked, that one too seedy.

There wasn't much money left, so she better make it last. She knew she was supposed to look at landmarks and discover this new city, but her heart wasn't in it. She just walked, aimlessly, thinking that something would stop her if it was important enough.

She passed by a subway. Hampstead. She ran down the stairs, then realized she didn't have any local currency and looked around for an exchange counter.

The map showed this suburb to be on a straight line from where the tube was. She started walking.

The day was well on its way to evening when she finally reached her goal: the Hampstead Heath. A park like you find only in England, at least that's what Jackie remembered reading about it some years ago.

It is still drizzling and Jackie is now soaked to the bone. She can't feel the damp. She walks up a trail which looks abandoned and sees a bench hiding among some trees and shrubs. Peace at last.

She takes her jacket off and finds a soiled, but dry sweater in her backpack. She trades the wet turtle neck, now clinging to her skin for the dry garment and sighs. The jacket is soaked, but she has no other, so she puts it back on, tucks the bag under her head, puts her feet up on the bench and sets out to die.

Dreams of paradise fail her. Instead, her daughters are calling out to her and Peter tries to stir her awake. She jumps up and finds a police officer shaking her back to reality.

His horse is only a few feet away and Jackie can feel how old it is in spite of the darkness.

"Excuse me, Madam, what are you doing here?" the man asks. Jackie stares at him and knows she has to summon her old self back if she doesn't want to be hauled in jail or worse. She smiles, and plays the American flake in London. "Wow, I'm sorry." She starts. "I was walking around earlier and, I guess I fell asleep. You see I walked from the city and just stopped to rest for a couple of minutes, but that was a while ago. What time is it?"

Jackie had learned over the years that to get out of trouble, she needed to take control. "It's three in the morning". The Bobby says. "Are you alright?"

"Of course." Jackie pursues in her most airy speech. "Wow, again, I don't know how that happened. I have to go back to my hotel. It's back in Kensington." She remembered that name from the subway map. "Do you know where I can find a cab or is the tube still working at this time?"

"Just follow me and I'll make sure you get a taxi up on the boulevard." She profusely thanks the officer, all the while wondering how she will get rid of him once out of the park. Most of the walk is done in total darkness. Jackie wonders how the officer found her. Probably accustomed to the city homeless population crashing here, he likely knows all the favorite spots.

They exit the park and enter the lit avenue where there is still life around bars and after hours restaurants. Jackie is hungry. It just occurred to her that she has had no food since the night before.

She watches as the officer flags a cab and waves as she gets in for the ride. "Thanks officer" she manages to say before asking the cabby to stop as soon as the uniformed man and his mount have turned the corner. "I have no English money." She tells him. I got here this morning and couldn't find an exchange counter. Just drop me off and I'll find one in the morning.

The driver sneaks a look to where Jackie is sitting. "I see. What kind of money do you have?" "French."

"No American?" he asks again. Jackie remembers a ten dollar bill left in her wallet. "Well, can I get to a train station with ten dollars?" she asks. "I'll take you as far as I can."

It turned out he took her as far as he thought the police couldn't find her and Jackie found herself back on the tube trail. The few hours spent on the bench had done little to give her some rest, and she now could feel what it was like to be without home or goal.

Looking at street signs and landmark triggered no memory of where anything was in spite of reading hundreds of novels built around this city. She just walked, straight, aimlessly, just assuming that once she can no longer walk, she'll just fall and be done with it.

Her mind was clear enough to wonder how all of this could have happened in such a short time. The story of the 'creation in seven days' started to make more sense. "If God could create a world in seven days, I could certainly destroy my life in…" she hesitated. She knew it was more than seven days, but couldn't remember clearly how many days had gone by.

She eventually saw a group of people, sitting around a fountain and looking like she must appear now, dirty and disheveled. She lied down on the grass surrounding the benches, seemingly trying to catch the first rays of sun, but, in fact, trying to escape into some dreamland.

She woke up as the sun was reaching its apex and wondered what time it was. Her watch was gone. How could someone take her watch without her noticing, she wondered. It didn't matter anyway. Time was no longer of the essence. She sat with her backpack between her crossed legs and just stared around her and decided she didn't like London. It felt something like New York without the American energy.

Jackie realized she was in no position to judge anything, let alone a whole city, but since nothing mattered, she would do it anyway. She searched her bag to see if she had any money left and found enough for probably another meal somewhere that cared about French money.

After more time spent staring and watching sad-looking people walking to wherever people went in this town, she picked herself and her bag up and started walking again. She passed by a restaurant garbage bin in an alley and spotted a croissant, still intact, presumably left by a patron already sated by a large breakfast; she looked around surreptitiously and grabbed it as fast as she could, then ran out of the alley just in case someone had seen her or followed her there.

Sitting on the steps of some old building, she enjoyed the buttery pastry, wishing there were more in some other alley. She wondered if they may be a whole sandwich after lunch had been consumed by the working population and her heart started beating faster. Maybe even a half full bottle of wine; but that was asking too much.

Jackie stayed on those steps for a while, not sure of what to do or where to go next. Someone threw money on her half open backpack. She was going to say "no, I'm not homeless," but then realized she was.

She started looking at people in a sad way like she had seen it done in her New York days when she told her daughter this could never happen to her. A lifetime ago. More passers-by threw money her way and as soon as she thought she had enough, she took it in and went into the first wine store on her path.

Hiding her bottle well into the backpack, she started walking again. Her steps brought her back to the train station where she thought she would find a clean bathroom and would look less conspicuous if she sat or even slept on a bench for a while. She eyed a couple of trash cans along the way, but nothing looked appetizing.

She was following the signs to the rest room when she saw a train was leaving for Brighton. Janice had told her about Brighton: this was the beach town where she had been stranded when her flight back to New York had been postponed for 24 hours, back in the times when airlines still cared about where their customers spent the night when they failed to fly.

Janice's description of the town made the idea of ending her journey on a beach something Jackie was now excited about.

She went to the ticket counter and asked how much the fare was. She showed her French currency and was handed a ticket together with enough change to get another bottle of wine.

Jackie's mood improved and she boarded the train, thinking she was finally converging to where she was supposed to be. She was going to the end. This was meant to be.

She starts drinking in the train, straight from the bottle, glad she is alone in the compartment. After a quick nap, she awakens to the conductor announcing the Brighton station. Jackie lands in the quiet town late in the afternoon.

Her first order of business is to find another place to buy wine, but then, she wonders if she should get something stronger. She almost drank the whole bottle in the train and still feels some awful pain inside that won't get numbed. "What do people drink to forget?" she wonders.

She briefly considers entering one of the bars on the main street. They are all crowded with men who appear to be in various stages of inebriation. She could have one of them buy her drinks. However, this would require socializing, talking, looking happy and she's not in the mood for that. "Enough of men, enough of life." She mutters to herself.

She sees a store window displaying various bottles and remembers that Scotch is not only an English drink, but also the one you always hear about on TV when a desperate man goes to drown his sorrows in a bar. Jackie looks at the bottles and counts her money: she can afford even the larger bottle and still have a bit of change. She almost cries for joy.

The beach is inviting, but with all those pebbles, it isn't the most comfortable place to sit, so Jackie wonders around town and finds a small alcove where she can finish her wine, and open her new bottle of whisky. She feels a burning as the liquid goes down, but it finds the spot where the pain was and now it's gone. She tilts her head back and smiles. Yes, this will do it. This will silence the demons. Hidden from view, she sits in a corner and moves her head from side to side to some obscure rhythm playing in her mind.

It is now dark. Over half the bottle is empty. She's not sure where she is, but suddenly the urge to talk to Janice has her stashing her bottle carefully back in her bag, standing and unsteadily trying to find a phone booth. She finally stumbles upon one near a pub which she realizes is closed. "Already past eleven" she thinks, wondering where she knows that from. No matter. What time is it in New York? She tries to count but the numbers are getting all mixed up in her head. She can't even remember if it's earlier or later. She manages to get in the booth and struggles to remember her friend's number. Her head is hitting the glass door, crying as she calls on her brain to summon up just this one last thing.

Jackie then sits on the floor of the booth looking through her bag for a pen to write down the few numbers she remembers and maybe create a spark of clarity in her mind. Twenty minutes have passed by the time she picks up the phone and manages to convey her wish to reverse the charges to call her friend in New York.

Her heart is beating. Jackie knows this is her last chance. If Janice isn't there, she can't even leave a message. Tears are streaming down, unchecked and unnoticed. Janice answers the phone and quickly accepts the charges. Peter has called her earlier that week to see if she had any news. He sounded casual, but there was something in his voice that put her on alert. Then she had received Jackie's letter this afternoon and started worrying about her friend.

"Janice, it's me" Jackie starts. "Sorry, I don't know what time it is there, but I had to talk to you.

"Hey sweetie, how are you doing?" Janice replies, realizing all is not well with her friend and deliberately keeping a calm voice to keep her on the line. "Where are you?"

"I'm in Brighton." Jackie replies. "Remember you told me you came here when I was in New York and you said it was a great little town. Well I'm here. I'm gonna go to the beach after I hang up so I can feel what you did that time. Remember the sound of the waves on the pebbles and everything. It sounded so good."

"But Jackie, it must be after midnight there. Don't you have a hotel to stay at where you can go?"

"No, no. I just… I just sort of been wondering around, you know. I'm sure some door will open here, I'm sure. Don't worry."

"When are you coming back?"

"I don't know." Jackie laughs a hysterical giggle. "I don't have a ticket anymore. It's just like me to lose something like that. I better go now. It's dark and I don't want anyone to see me. I miss you Jan." Jackie hangs up, not hearing her friends' plea to stay on the line and talk.

She takes a swig out of the bottle and aims for the beach. There, she finds a small boat to hide behind and takes whatever clothes she can find to make a bed over the hard stones. She stares at the ocean, as if she were looking in a mirror. It is black with the occasional foam gleaming under the half moon. She smiles, and drinks until there is no more and her head finds the ground where she closes her eyes.

Jackie wakes up the next morning and cannot lift her head. The ground is hard and her body aching in its every muscle.

She wonders what day or what time it is. She hasn't thought about the day since she left Paris, or maybe she did but she can't remember. She remembers her watch is gone. Peter gave her that watch for their anniversary last year. It doesn't matter. The sun is more than half-way up in the sky. She figures close to noon.

She looks down at herself; her clothes are rumpled and torn in places. She touches her messy and now dirty hair; she thinks she smells and, as if awaking from a dream, puzzles on how she arrived here.

Her head is in a daze of morning confusion and she wonders what she must do next. Jackie cannot remember yesterday but she feels there wasn't supposed to be a today.

She hears footsteps behind her. Not wanting any attention, she crouches on the ground and purposely looks the other way.

"Jackie."

Her whole body responds to the call. Her name hadn't been spoken quite this way in years. She turns and sees Tommy standing near her, still handsome in a bald sort of way, smiling his sad looking smile, the one she so often tried to make happy. She didn't remember him being so short.

She turns back and he sits next to her. "What happened Jackie?"

She shrugs and stares at the sea, now looking grayer in the fall sunlight.

"You know I've missed you over the last few years. We were good for each other. I never could find a friend like you. I wish I could have been a better husband, a better father." He pauses, thinking about all the pain they had caused each other. "I was hurt for a long time. I'm still hurt, I think.' The sad smile again.

She turns toward him and looks at this man, the father of her children, who now stands thousands of miles from home taking about their lives.

"Janice called me yesterday. I hadn't heard from her in years, but for some reason she called me. She thought maybe I could help somehow. I jumped on the first plane out and here I am. You probably didn't know I could do things like that" he adds trying in vain to lighten the mood. "I don't know what to say, I just want you to know I'm here."

They both turn to the water, the occasional stroller ignoring this unusual pair, sitting on the cool morning pebbles, still, not talking, just staring.

"I wish I had been there for you. At the time, I was so self-involved; I couldn't see the forest for the trees. I always thought you were so strong, nothing could break you. I knew you had to be responsible for everything that happened because you made all the decisions. I'm sorry. I learned over the last years how to love without depending on someone, I learned how to lean on someone without taking the life away from her. I wish I'd known that when I knew you."

She shrugged again, not knowing what to say to this ghost from her past, coming to haunt her on this desperate path to self-destruction she had been following for the last while. There was a soft glow from his voice which awakened something Jackie had thought was gone long ago: the teenage romantic sleeping deep inside her. She knew she could never love this man again, but the soft feeling she felt was one she wanted to keep.

"Call home." He said. She turns to face him. "Call home" he repeated. "Peter loves you and I'm sure he's worried about you; the girls still need you." He slowly stands and offers his hand out to her. She looks, hesitates then takes it. "I think I'm ready now." She says.

##

JULIE

Saturday A.M. Welcome to fifty, well, tomorrow, but still. Yeah, right! What does it really mean? It's just another day. Then, why do I feel like such shit?

I just got this journal from a colleague at work yesterday who laughingly implied I should start writing things down before my memory fails. I hate those so-called 'old' jokes. I don't find them amusing, especially coming from a male. In fact they are not only inappropriate, they are downright sexist. If the old guys I work with didn't have their young assistants, they wouldn't remember where their car is parked. After all, men 'lose it' far earlier than women do and many completely fall apart if their wives go first, whereas most of us, women, are self-sufficient and stay alert and involved to the bitter end... so there.

Anyway, enough of this. I just thought, why not use it? It's been a while, like 35 years, since I've written in a diary, but, I don't know, I just feel like starting again.

My coffee is cold. The golf course is already crawling with the retired crowd, all decked out in pastel shorts and shirts, teeing-off. Golf is such serious business here but when you think of it, the dress is oh so tacky. (Do I look like that too?) What would people do without the country club? That's were we all meet, swim, play tennis, socialize and manage to avoid any contact with people remotely poorer than us. For some reason, this life felt so right yesterday, but it seems pathetic this morning. My former-hippy-artist-ecologically golf-hating, politically correct sister Carrie would be proud of me!

Work. Golf. Tennis. Social functions. Family. Money. That pretty much summarizes it. I wonder what my 20 year old self would say if she saw what has happened to me. Scary thought, but all in all, I think she'd be pleased. I always wanted 'stuff', so now I have a lot of 'stuff'!

When we built this house five years ago, being on the golf course was Richard's ultimate dream. Who needs four bedrooms the size of comfortable board rooms, four bathrooms where you could do your morning calisthenics, a nanny suite on the main floor, towers and cornices, bricks and stones, all sitting just about right on the first green? I thought I did! Now I only see the convenience of being able to walk home when we're drunk.

Come to think of it, we moved here just before Jake was born. God, I didn't expect another kid. I'm not even sure I wanted another kid. Actually I'm sure I didn't, but Richard decided it was a great idea and that we needed more room, so here we are. I can't believe we've been married almost 30 years. Life has just gone by so fast, it's like I want the world to slow down so I can look back and see how I missed my stop. I'd always earned more than Richard and that was fine, but when he turned into a computer geek in the mid-eighties after years of bean counting, his newfound calling brought us up to the "Westchester County monument to the American Dream house" family income level. OK, I still make more than him, but it doesn't matter so much anymore.

Thirty years. Takes me back to college when I got pregnant for Josée. I wasn't sure I wanted her either at the time, but here she is now, 29 years old, a dentist for God' sake, and married with, of all people, our BMW mechanic. Jon is nice enough, but he lacks in the sophistication department. So I'm a snob. Sue me. Funny how the only one of our kids who was really planned and wanted, is turning into such a, and I hate to say that being his mother, loser. Christopher, barely out of high school, is, for all intents and purposes following some head-banger (is this expression still in?) band around the country while pretending to go to community college.

On the outside, we all look sane enough, but digging in, I think we probably would fit in with the best of dysfunctional families. We say all is well, we act all is well, but there is nothing behind that facade. It's like there is a hole inside of me the size of the Grand Canyon and nothing to fill it with. The 'stuff' doesn't seem to work anymore. Funny, I just wrote this, and realized it took years for the canyon to form. How long has my 'soul' been eroding?

I just took a look at the markets in the paper this morning and, as usual, I feel a pit at the bottom of my stomach: every day, I wonder if I'll come home still employed or not. So much for the Wall Street 'power career' thing. It just takes a few terrorists, or a bad president, or even the rumor of a recession to make everything I worked for tumble into ruins. Don't know why, but I somehow don't care this morning. This whole American Dream thing is turning into a fucking nightmare of mortgages, junk food and everyone looking at me for… I'm not even sure what for.

I better get some fresh coffee on before the 'mob' descends on me. Idea: have a button you can push to turn your family off and on. Interesting concept.

##

JULIE

Monday A.M. I can't believe it's 10:30. I haven't slept so late in years. Even the smell of coffee is making me nauseous. My brain is in a fog; I can barely see the paper I'm trying to write on.

Richard must have left for work early. I didn't hear a thing. Who knows, maybe he went home with someone else last night. At this point, I really couldn't care less. My head is pounding behind my eyes and I think I'll throw up. Dying last night would have been nice. What a nice way to go: half a century and who knows how many pink drinks later...

For some reason, the room is spinning out of control... Just took a deep breath, swallowed a couple of aspirins, and am trying to clear my head. The house is so quiet; I wonder where every one is. My gosh, it's Monday. I should be at work. What is wrong with me?

Last night was my long awaited, 'surprise' birthday party. The whole clan, plus at least 50 of our 'closest' friends ganged up on me at the country club.

So I'm 50. What's the big deal? I got more chocolate and flowers than anyone has any need for, and those silly, supposedly funny cards with comments about old age or menopause really got old (pun intended) after a while. A good thing I'm good at plastering this genuine-looking smile on my face, no matter what I'm thinking which, at the time was along the lines of "what the hell am I doing here?"

Richard was enjoying himself. He was so ebullient I couldn't tell exactly who he was talking to or, worse still, what he was talking about. When I came in, he grabbed me around the shoulder and snuck an envelope in my pants pocket. Everyone was already in high spirits, and I returned more hugs and phony pecking kisses than I care to remember.

Jake was being the perfect little boy, telling anyone who would listen, how he was the best in his piano class and the guests, in turn, were drooling and doting on his miniature manly body. He is way too serious for his age; prissy may even be a better word. By 10 o'clock, Sandra was nowhere to be found. As his nanny, she should have known it was way past his bedtime and taken him home. I didn't think I should be the one to do it! I finally found her, relaxing with a glass of wine with some guy I didn't know, and had her drag Jake home. He looked like a spoiled prince retiring for the night!

Josée and Jon were sitting at a table near the exit, glancing at the clock, looking for an appropriate time to leave. I considered walking over, but changed my mind: Hell, it was my birthday after all. They should come and talk to me.

Of course, Christopher had run off as soon as politely possible but strangely enough, I saw him walk back through the garden doors, with a gleam in his eyes. No surprise there either. I know his newfound glee was not caused by the joy of seeing me turn fifty.

I wish I'd seen a friend there. I mean there were lots of familiar faces, but no one I wanted to start a conversation with. Hum, do I have any friends or just acquaintances?" Something to think about. Anyway, I zeroed-in on the bar and my favorite bar tender, sexy Gino. I always imagine that if I had bummed around Europe after college, there would have been a Gino to seduce me out of my girlhood. He had probably 'done' all of the Westchester housewives plus his share of divorcees, widows, well, pretty much any female within a 5-mile radius, he really wasn't my type but I did like to flirt with him.

He kept the strange colorful drinks with parasols coming and I wish I could remember how I eventually got home.

Did I ever look into the envelope Richard gave me? If I did, I don't remember! I guess I better take a peek; looks like it's been sitting on the counter all night.

Hey, wild. It's a certificate for two weeks of pampering and stuff in one of those spas somewhere in Colorado. Cool. God, I feel like shit.

The coffee is tepid and stale; I think it burned at the bottom of the pot or something. To hell with it. I'm going back to bed and screw work. Maybe I can sleep until my next birthday.

"Richard,

Thank you for a great birthday party last night. I wish I hadn't had so much to drink and hope I didn't insult anyone nor do anything stupid during the period, which, at this time, is totally obscured from my conscious mind.

I found your present in my pocket and decided to take advantage of it and leave today. I thought driving all the way there would do me good. Don't ask why. I want to thank you and hope you understand that I need this time now and will hopefully come back a better person.

Ask Josée if she can move in with Jon for a while to help out with Jake.

Don't forget to pay Sandra on Thursday and leave money on the table for Alice when she comes to clean the house next Monday. Also, can you call work for me and say I'm sick or whatever you want, so they don't think I died?

Love,

Julie."

##

Monday, later… I'm happy I brought this silly journal. I feel like I want to share my thoughts, but can't think of anyone I want to share them with. This will do.

This morning, I really intended to sleep, but for some reason, as soon as I got upstairs, I guess the aspirins kicked in and I got an urge to just take off. I got dressed, packed a couple of things, wrote a note for Richard and started to drive due west. Unfortunately, it didn't take long before the hangover came back to haunt me. I had to stop and chow down on some fast food so my stomach would be nicely coated with fat and ignore whatever else was ailing it.

In any case, I never even made it out of Pennsylvania. I stopped at this seedy motel and am now wondering what the hell happened and, why did I stop in this dive!

Maybe I'll go home tomorrow. Maybe this is all crazy. I want to be left alone, but I miss my cell phone. I want to run away, but I'd like to take a long bath in my Jacuzzi tub. Why did I do such a silly thing… and I'm not even talking about work. I guess I could go to that spa, since this is where Richard thinks I am over the next two weeks, but... nah... Too much like the country club.

Thank heavens for those PM pills I had the presence of mind to pack. I'm going under.

Tuesday: On the road again, having lunch. I decided I'm definitely not going home and most certainly not to the spa. I woke up and saw my life as a B movie or one of those boring sitcoms, and decided to turn the TV off. I know I should feel more than this, but I don't.

I took as much as I could from my bank account at a gas station ATM. Just in case... I'll send a postcard to the kids. Maybe I can find one by the cash register with palm trees and sand to throw them off!

Wednesday: Another Bates Motel night. I drove all day yesterday and just stopped for lunch in this all but ghost town, save for a gas station, a greasy diner and a couple of non-descript stores and houses. I'm in the mountains now, I have no clue where. I wish I'd paid more attention in my geography class. I've probably flown over these hills a millions times, but I've never favored long driving vacations, so any uninteresting parts of the country are mysteries to me. I'm thinking of holing out here for a while.

Funny how I am totally numb, like I never had a life before. I looked at the night table and its 60's vintage phone, a 'princess,' we used to call it, and am almost tempted to call home. No, they'll ask too many questions, ones I'm not ready to answer yet, not even to myself and besides, I'm an awful liar. I did send a postcard though; no palm tress, but one of those 'could be from anywhere types' just to say I'm OK.

I was chatting with a woman while filling the tank up in town today. She says she's got a cabin she could rent for a while. I'm seriously considering taking her up on the offer. I'll sleep on it once the raucous noises stop below me since this room is on top of the bar (is this a step up or down from Bates?)

Thursday: Forget about the driving, I decided to stick around here, far enough from home, and so unlike the type of climate I favor, no one would ever think of coming here to find me.

The cabin turned out to be miles from the town. From tar, to gravel, to dirt, I thought I was lost for a while, but then, there it was, a tiny shack, wind passing through the wooden slates, no bathroom to talk about, actually none inside the premises, only a cot, a rudimentary sink, the kind that needs to be pumped up, a wood stove, a butane burner (I still haven't figured out how that works and I don't think there is any gas in the tank), a home-made table and matching chairs. No electricity, no TV.

So much for the refrigeration-required provisions I bought in town. Oh well, the temperature outside should be cold enough to accommodate the stuff… unless some animal finds it first. Hum, the car! I'll use the trunk as a refrigerator: I am oh, so clever! I love it.

Now I see why I've been toting these silly shoulder-hanging picnic chairs and Mexican blankets in my car all this time. They'll be the most comfortable pieces of furniture here and the warmest bed cover. I better get busy getting some wood so I can keep relatively warm tonight. It may be Indian summer back home, but here, fall is definitely in full deployment.

Friday: God, was I ever unprepared for this. I have to get back to town for more practical provisions, like candles, oil for the lamps and tons of butane. Am I doing the right thing? I've been so busy thinking of myself, I find it hard to be objective. Well, gotta go.

7:30 PM. Wow. I just realized I was still running on the old momentum. It feels really silly here. One chair for sitting, the other for my feet and I find myself finally relaxing. I had to get some screw-top wine, but it's better than nothing. The cabin faces west and, in spite of the forest around it, I can see a sunset through the branches in place of where the leaves used to be. Mostly oaks, birches and cedars, so not too much in terms of fall colors. I can just sit and stare. I have no words to write.

Monday: I can't believe I've been gone a week. I spent the weekend covering up the cracks in the wall. Saturday, I went back to town for books, warm pants, flannel shirt, a parka and some boots.

Funny how New York never seems that cold, even in the winter. Maybe it's the starting off in the garage at home and ending up in another, larger one downtown. I find myself sleeping in my clothes. Why didn't I think of that before? Makes getting up a whole lot easier. Christopher used to do that as a teenager and I always thought it was only to annoy me. Stuff you learn from your kids!

Tuesday: I'm running out of wood, but haven't figured out how to chop some more yet. Desperation being the mother of invention, I'm confident I'll learn quickly once I start freezing. A few snow flakes have fallen earlier this morning and some ominous clouds lurch on the horizon. I'm still trying to feel something beyond the fact that I'm glad I'm here, but don't really know why. I really don't. It's like I'm in a play and just go through the motions without being emotionally involved. Just occurred to me that if it snows, the state plows probably don't make it this far. Interesting.

Later: I have never heard such silence before. A blanket of snow covers the road and it seems like I'm the only living creature left in the world. A white glow comes from the window where the moon is reflected in the new landscape. I used to run in the new snow to show it who was in control, but not now. It needs to be alone and stay in its virgin state for a while. It's like I've never seen snow before.

Strange how well I've been sleeping here. I could get used to that. I find myself forgetting what time it is and have been following the natural rise and fall of daylight over the last few days. I'm starting to recapture some feelings from a past I don't even remember.

White, blue
Christmas landscape
Branches heavy with their burden of snow.
Black limbs, extending white arms to their neighbors.

Some animal just peeked out from behind a cedar and quickly disappeared back in the woods.

There is life after all. I still don't want to move. I wrap the blanket around my shoulders

##

Wednesday: I slept in the chair all night. My back is killing me. This is the first time I ever do something like that. I'm hungry for toasts and eggs. Maybe I'll get a couple of chickens. I noticed a little hen house near the woodshed. Talking about which, I'll go and gather some kindling and good sized dead branches for the fire. Hope I can find some dry ones. Still not up to chopping.

Later… The snow is melting. I guess it's too early for it to settle down and stick. I have a decision to make: if I stay any longer, I risk being stranded for days, if not weeks once winter sets in. If I leave, where do I go? If I don't report back home, they'll be looking for me. What do I do? I need a sign.

Later: I just came in from a walk in the snow. It's not the crispy type of a mid winter fall, nor the mushy type of a spring storm. It's different. It's my snow. Well, I just looked out and it's now my mud. I wonder how long the roads take to dry up? The temperature has gone back up to the fifties. Washing my hair is what I find the hardest. Maybe I'll just braid it tight and let it go for a while.

##

Thursday: It has been raining since last night. The mud is turning into lumpy gravy, flowing down the road like lava from an angry volcano. I moved the car to higher grounds. I should have used Richard's 4 X 4. I hate the gas guzzling beast, but my Beamer isn't much good to me here! The cloud cover is massive and there is no break in sight. I'm just burning up wood and staying cozy by the fire. How did I ever find time or the energy for that other life? I've taken to eating soup everyday: Every morning, I put piles of vegetables in a pot, add water and tomato juice and just keep it on the stove so I can eat whenever I feel the need. I made some bread yesterday: OK it was a mix, but considering I have a one-temperature-fits-all oven, it turned out quite well. The smell was enough to keep me happy for hours.

Friday: More rain. For all intents and purposes, I'm stuck here until something up there dries up the road. I am getting a little weary.

Saturday. I was awakened this morning with a bang… literally. Very unnerving. Things have dried up a bit, so I might just chance it down to town later. I'd hate to think people are shooting stuff around me. Really freaks me out.

Later… I looked at the road this afternoon and thought, no, not going to happen. It's still too muddy.

The crackling fire and smell of soup is lulling me into almost a meditative state. I can't read. I just find myself thinking about stuff like: how can I reverse Jake's almost grown-up behavior? He should be allowed to be a kid and just have fun. How can I be fifty with a five year old son? How can I convince Christopher to stop and take stock of his life? Mostly, I wonder how I can make up for some many years lost keeping my daughter on the sideline of my life. My brain is spinning around like a top, not stopping long enough at any crossroad to produce rational thoughts. And Richard. What is left of our marriage? We're comfortable, is all I can think about it. No sparks, not excitement. Is comfortable enough? It is for him I guess. What I'd like is to actually be passionate about all this. Like Carrie would be. I never seem to be able to care enough. I'm so fucking methodical, logical and always doing the rational thing… until now, I guess… and still…

The shots are still ringing in my ears. Made me feel very uncomfortable. I hope the road is dry enough tomorrow. I'll be running out of fresh food soon.

Sunday. I didn't sleep well last night. It's like my body is 'fibrillating'. There are spring-like nerves going up and down, back and forth in my limbs. I don't like this. I tried to mentally chant the mantra I use when we meditate in Yoga class, something which usually helps me sleep, but it didn't work.

Well, at least it hasn't rained overnight, but the clouds are sort of threatening. Rain or Snow? It just occurred to me that this is probably hunting season in this area. The thought of potentially drunken armed men coming within earshot of the cabin adds to this dreadful feeling. The clouds don't help. I haven't seen the sun in a while. I wonder what everyone is doing at home. I'm restless for the first time since I got here.

I should go out and get some wood, but for some reason I dread the thought. I have to get to town. Well, an hour down, an hour back up, it's almost one o'clock. If I don't go now, I never will. Here goes nothing.

Later. I'm writing, shabby curtains closed and by candlelight. If anyone ever finds this, know that it is OK. I had a great life and don't need anymore time. I've accomplished what I had set out to do, even thought, looking back, I may have sold, or at any rate, leased my soul to the devil. As I always said "There are a lot of indispensable people in the cemetery". So there. Be happy and remember the 'me' you all liked best. Wish I knew which 'me' that was… if I get out of here in one piece, I'll be sure to ask.

I left the cabin this afternoon, determined to go into town. Took me the better part of half an hour just to climb up the slippery dirt road and by the time I got there, it was obvious that my car was no match for this mud, which in places went over my boots. I hushed the panic that was rising in my chest and decided to chance it down the hill. Most of the way to town was downhill and, maybe the road would be dryer father down.

It started well enough and I was relieved to find myself moving forward while trying to keep from sliding down the hill too fast. Maybe the car was worth the small fortune I paid for it after all. I passed the cabin and thought 'downhill from here'. Yeah, fat chance. I had forgotten about the little valley about 2 miles down. Nice to go down to, but the hill going back up wouldn't have it. I backed up, tried again, went back and forth at least half a dozen times. I finally had to give up when the tires got completely buried in the slimy, muddy ruts. I didn't even make it to the gravel. OK, I cried. Not sure if it was plain frustration, discouragement or raw panic.

By that time my boots were one with the road and I had to make the painful decision to walk back and wait it out. I guess canned food and soda keep a lot of other people alive, so a couple of days on that diet wouldn't hurt me. Unfortunately, the sky showed no promise of respite from the threatening clouds and the wind had that bitter sweet quality of a draft going through the bathroom window when you're in the shower. I started to walk back, and it was almost dark when I finally rounded the last corner near the cabin.

I was breathing easier, thinking of a warm fire and a hot bowl of canned beans, when I noticed some red at the corner of my eyes. I stopped short and saw two men coming out of the woods behind the cabin.

They were laughing, shot gun on their shoulder, bright shirts filled with mud, cans of beer in hand. The days-old beard and ratty old caps brought visions of the book 'Deliverance" which I had read in college. I decided to lay low behind some bushes and wait.

Did I say it was almost freezing by then? Well, it was. I pulled the hood of my parka tight around my head and tied it high over my chin. My hands weren't so lucky and, as wet as my gloves were, they started to freeze. I could hear clamor from my cabin and feared they may stay there all night. Smoke rose out of the chimney and I was resigned to a certain death from exposure. I wondered if I should I go back to the car and heat it up but couldn't move. By then, my brain had turned into that of prey, fearing its predator. I couldn't make any sensible decision.

I tried to tell myself that these guys were probably accountant types who just came up for the weekend and wouldn't hurt me. Maybe we'd all be laughing about it. Didn't work. I couldn't even make the steps that would lead me to the cabin and, what I was sure of by then is certain death, probably preceded by rape and torture. What is wrong with me?

It was pitched black when the men finally decided to go, leaving a trail of light after them to the back of the cabin and the path they had descended from. I waited for what seemed like hours, but they didn't come back.

I snuck back in, petrified that they should return.

There were ambers in the grate and I sat as close as I could without burning my coat and peeled off my boots. My feet were numb. I considered adding more wood, but didn't want anyone to know I was here, so I just sucked in as much heat as I could from that source before it was consumed. I lit candles, remembering that they can heat a small space if required. I also got the butane burner going and slowly started to thaw out.

They drank the bottle of wine I opened last night. I quietly reached for a bag where I had stashed some cookies, but it was empty.

I crawled to the bed and saw that they hadn't found my carry-all, stored under the cot. My journal was still in it and, not that it matters much now, but my money was also still there. So, here I am, trying to warm my fingers on the candle and writing what may well be my last thoughts.

I feel here that I should say something significant, but all I can think about is that I was cheated by life. Or is it by my own American dream folly? I've had it all. No, I have never had freedom. Even the last two weeks. Freedom should mean being free from fear, free to live, never second-guessing what others think, and all of this in peace. Boy, I'm turning into a regular philosopher.

I always looked at other women and thought "I'm liberated", "I'm free". Not. I'm still waiting for that illusive promotion that will take me into the 'old boys' club. I got lulled by the money, the 'stuff', the trappings, but I'm just as oppressed, except at a higher level. I'm a fraud.

Richard can go back and forth in his career and everyone thinks of him as courageous and brilliant. Me, I'm just safe. If I had chosen a different path at a different time, I would have been discouraged to do it. Women are not rewarded when they take risks or chances. They are regarded as quitters and rarely find anyone willing to go along with their new vision, unless, of course, their newfound calling is that of a stay-at-home wife and mother!

Funny I just got a clear mental view of what someone would see if they walked in right now. Me, crunched up on the floor, a couple of candles burning, making small shivering shadows around each other, and a palpable fear I'm trying to hide behind this endless chain of words. Pathetic. Damn it's cold in here.

##

Monday. I guess I eventually fell asleep on the floor. My body is a mess of aches and pains. I chanced a look outside and was blinded by a sky so blue it hurt. The sun hasn't peaked from behind the mountain behind me, but it looks like it soon will.

What a difference morning makes. Not that much actually. My entire being hurts and wants to be out of here, but I am conscious that I will faint half-way back if I don't eat. The guys from yesterday didn't take the cans, but I don't have time for this. Dry cereals it is. I crammed my travel bag with a blanket, matches, candles, and leftover cereals. The chairs and everything else will just have to stay. My boots are crusty from the mud and are hard to slip back on. There won't be much warmth there. I'm hiding this journal in a secret pocket inside the parka. It should be safe.

##

Saturday. Every day that I have been back, I have wanted to write but I could only stare at the blank page and eventually close the diary. After this, I will probably never write in it again.

Walking to the car on Monday was a painful experience. The sun helped as a psychological illusion of warmth, but it was in fact ice cold. By the time I took stock of the BMW's status, it was all but rooted in the frozen ground. As luck or irony would have it, this frozen ground was what the car needed to work its way out of the ruts. The ride was rough, but since I anticipated to be walking all the way to town, it felt as smooth as a boat ride in Central Park.

I didn't stop as I drove through town. I had already paid a month's worth of rent and would call the woman later when enough distance was put between me and this mountain. I drove what must have been five hours when my body reminded me that it needed food and sleep. As soon as a larger town showed more civilized potential, I stopped at the largest and most comfortable-looking hotel I could see.

After a long bath, and ordering the most expensive meal on the room service menu, I called home.

Richard answered. "How was the spa?" he said. I started laughing uncontrollably and, puzzled but amused, he humored me with a giggle. "Why are you laughing so hard?"

He couldn't know that all this time I thought my family had sent search parties for me. He wouldn't understand how, even in my strongest craving for quitting this life, I still believed someone would contact the spa to see if I had made it there and was still alive. He hadn't even noticed the bank balance.

I wonder how long it would have been before they had noticed if I had been killed by the hunters or mauled by a black bear. I just told Richard I'd be back late the next day and hung up. I couldn't stop laughing. Pathetic.

I called room service and asked to add an extra dry Crown Royal Manhattan and a bottle of expensive French wine to my order, as well as a double shot of Amaretto. Turned the TV on to HBO and watched some movie about... well, I'm not sure I remember.

I woke up on Tuesday, no longer laughing and back to the pounding headache and nausea of two weeks ago.

All in all, I think, I love the power career, the nanny, the housekeeper, the country club. I even love the fact that Jake may personally request boarding school before he's ten and that Christopher will likely need me forever to bail him out of whatever trouble he's in. Josée, well I'll have to think about her. Richard... we're used to each other. Nothing wrong with that. I guess well see what happens there. In the meantime, I'm back. I'm home. I am not a new person: no one changes so much, (sorry, Carrie.) But now I know I can dig just a little deeper and bring some added dimension to my life. Fifty? So what? Another fifty to go and I'm ready. Watch out ol'boys, 'cause Julie's coming back.

##

7

PATRICIA

She had not eaten in three days. Not since the funeral. She just sat on what used to be Bill's favorite recliner, staring at a blank television screen.

Next week, Pat was crossing the infamous 'fifty yard line', an event which may have gone almost unnoticed until now. As if losing her husband wasn't stressful enough. Twenty years is how long Pat had been living side by side with a man she had learned to lean on and find comfort with.

No matter that Bill's life consisted of working at an insignificant job in a mediocre law firm and watching inane television programs. He was her rock. Pat's job was not glamorous either so their relationship was a perfect fit. Like old comfortable shoes or an abused, favorite chair. They believed this is what love was and were content with their lives.

"That's about it" thought Pat, remembering their fist date of movie and pizza followed by weekly Friday night dinner at a local eatery. Saturdays were the nights when she cooked for them and when he always brought the latest video release. It was two months before he started staying over, which led to the new ritual of a Sunday walk in the park after which they parted ways until the morning when they would see each other again at the office.

At the time, Bill was a little over 35, a bit pudgy and showed the beginning of early balding. She was quite shapeless and admittedly plain. They were a perfect match or so everyone where they worked thought. When Bill proposed, no one was surprised as if this was just meant to be.

Pat and Bill had something else in common: they both lacked any close friends or, in fact, any friends at all, so they kept each other company day in and day out. After they were married, vacations and holidays were just extensions of nights and weekends.

Now she was alone. Bill's whole office staff had showed up for the funeral and although she had quit her job there and moved on to a new law firm after their marriage, Pat still knew most of them from attending yearly Christmas parties. No one from her firm had come. She never got close to anyone there, so her co-workers barely noticed her frequent absences while Bill was sick and the news of his death was received with the appropriate respect, but no more.

At the funeral, she had gone through the motions of being the bereaved widow. Then, back home, she served hors-d'oeuvres to his colleagues, and later called her own boss to let him know not to expect her back in the office for a while. That's when she had stumbled onto Bill's chair and filled it with her own body, waiting for, not really sure what she was waiting for.

She was trying to make sense of life, make sense of his death. The hospice had been a peacefully stressful place for him to die. Lung cancer. Not even a smoker... well anymore that is. No hope. Now what? She had had no time to get used to his leaving her, not enough time to plan or figure out how to feel.

She knew Bill had planned a special dinner at the finest restaurant in town for her fiftieth birthday, like the one she had surprised him with five years earlier when it had been his turn to reach the half century mark. The dinner was supposed to be a surprise, but they knew each other so well, they could no longer keep secrets from one another.

Bill had never told her about his finances, nor had Pat ever told him of hers: they paid the household expenses out of a common account, but neither seemed to care what the other was doing with what was left, if anything. They had enough to live on, enjoyed their all paid for, little brick bungalow with its cozy charm and put aside a bit every month for when one of the cars would have to be replaced.

In twenty years, they had been on one vacation to Myrtle Beach but neither cared for the beach, so they tacitly decided that movies at home and Fourth of July fireworks were more satisfying than spending hours in a car just to have sand thrown at you by unruly kids on a hot and sticky shore. Neither could swim. They talked about going to the mountains once, but the idea dwindled away for lack of interest.

Theirs was not a passionate relationship, but both were satisfied with the comfort they had attained in their intimacy. As simple as their life together was, they were happy and never yearned for anything or anyone else.

In Pat's mind, they should have gone on until one of them died of old age and the other would follow soon after. After meeting Bill, she had never foreseen being fifty, alone and faced with a blank screen as the rest of her life.

She visualized herself now, sitting on the recliner, wearing the same clothes she had worn to the funeral, probably smelling like death herself and wondered if you could just die by wishing it so hard. She needed an excuse to rise and live, but couldn't find one.

##

Norman walked into Bill's office, looked around and wondered how someone could work somewhere for almost thirty years and leave nothing that gave away his uniqueness or personality. Bill was the guy no one ever saw. He was well liked and could be relied on to research cases and to write excellent briefs for the other lawyers. While Bill was a bona fide lawyer himself, the idea of his achieving partner status had never crossed anyone's mind, not even Bill's.

Norman felt like an intruder, but he had been told by management that the office, kept available during Bill's illness, now had to be vacated within a week and no one had talked to Patricia about picking up his personal effects. This would fall upon Norman to call her when he was done. Everyone in the office had commented on how Pat had looked so calm and showed no emotions one way or the other, how perfect the ceremony and burial had been and how great the food was.

Bill's desk itself was neat, devoid of personal photos or mementos. The file cabinets were crammed with reference notes Bill had painstakingly taken over the course of his career. Thousands of pages, carefully written and classified for posterity. Norman wondered if anyone had ever used much of this extensive research and assumed much of it would have to be shredded since they contained confidential information which should have been, by law, destroyed years ago.

Going through the desk drawers didn't reveal anymore of Bill's character, but there were personal files that would have to be given to the widow. Letters, bills, investment documents and, soon he found a will. It was dated back a few years, but properly notarized, signed and looked valid. Of course the firm would take care of this legal document and probate for their employee's widow, but she would have to come into the office.

##

The phone rang. Pat stirred in Bill's chair and wondered if she should just let it ring. She smiled, remembering how her husband never answered the phone and refused to have one he could reach from his favorite chair. "It can't be that important" he used say, "and if it is, they'll call back." They never did. Most calls were from telemarketers or wrong numbers. Her family was long gone and, as far as she knew, Bill was also alone in the world. She remembered he had mentioned that his father, an army man, had died in the Korean War and his mom of cancer only a few years later. He had no brothers or sisters that she knew of.

His education had been done under the GI Bill and he had found himself a comfortable niche in the world which had been complete once he married Pat.

She finally rose with a "middle aged grunt" as Bill used to refer to the noise she made when rising from a comfortable seat, and reached for the phone.

##

Pat lingered in the shower for almost an hour, forgetting her normal frugality, feeling the hot water caress her body as if for the first time. A pleasant tingling was going through her and she wanted it to last for as long as she could. This was the first pleasant feeling she was having since Bill was diagnosed with cancer only a few months ago. She put on her best business suit and drove downtown.

By three o'clock, Pat was in front of the early twentieth century house where she and Bill had first laid eyes on each other. She tried to remember when she had climbed these stairs last. Had to be at least ten years. Christmas parties were always held in a local restaurant. Save for fresh paint and newly paved walk, nothing had changed.

The receptionist greeted her with a somber look and talked to her as thought she was an old friend. She called Norman to the reception area and the young man shyly exchanged a handshake with the widow before preceding her to the conference room. He motioned her to sit by his side at the long, angular table while another member of the staff was shuffling through some papers, getting ready to read the will.

Bill's testament was simple, to the point, and the only surprise it held was that Pat was now finding herself a moderately wealthy woman. Between investments and life insurance, Bill had made sure she was well taken care of, or perhaps, Pat reflected, smiling to herself, he thought he could take it with him.

She was in no mood for socializing so, as soon as she saw a way out, Pat thanked them, left them with banking, tax and whatever other information and instructions necessary to process all of these documents and left as she came with very few words spoken and a briefcase filled with the private papers she would have to study when she got home.

Pat walked into her house and couldn't believe the mess she saw. She changed into work pants and started cleaning up the clutter. The dirty dishes left in the kitchen after the funeral were still in the sink. After the house was back to its usual tidiness, she started idly going through some of the personal notes found in Bill's desk. It was after midnight when she finally went to bed, and, for the first time in weeks, had a dreamless night.

##

The interstate was quiet at this time of morning. A small suitcase packed at dawn, Pat had filled up the tank with gas and started on what she though of as her 'half-century pilgrimage'. The need had been triggered last night while she was reading through Bill's files and she had determined to fill the gap between her present and her past once and for all.

The sun was just rising over the horizon. She caught glimpses of it in her rearview mirror. A good omen, she though.

"Over thirty years. Has it already been that long?" Pat mused while settling for the long drive. Her mind went back to that other sunrise three decades ago when she had last seen her childhood home. The memory of that morning overwhelmed her like a giant wave: she had not allowed her past to surface in all these years but was ready for it now.

##

The sun had been just as bright that morning. Pat had watched it rise from the kitchen window after a sleepless night. The house was quiet.

After her mother died from cancer, her father had decreed that there would be no more pets allowed in the house. Pat missed her Cookie, a tabby her mom had rescued as a kitten from the jaws of a neighbor's dog and who had kept Pat company every night since she was old enough to remember. Unaccustomed to outdoor living, the tabby had been hit by a truck on the road a short time after and was never replaced.

Only she, her older sister Shelly and her father lived in the farmhouse now and Shelly had gone to bed early after her chores. Late last night, Pat had seen her dad turn into the driveway, swerve erratically, park his truck at the back door, then crash on the living couch to sleep-off a hangover. He seemed to be doing that a lot lately.

Pat had a painful secret, Pat was pregnant. She had waited to be sure and was so excited when she was told that 'the rabbit died', she couldn't wait to rush over to her boyfriend's house to tell him. They would get married and she would be the best wife ever. She wanted a girl, but it didn't matter if it turned out to be a boy. She would love whatever God sent her. She was almost 18, so it wasn't like she was too young to get married. She ran the mile that separated her from her lover's house, knocked on his door and called out. He seemed surprised and not as pleased to see her as she had wished, but she knew that when he would find out about the baby, he would be happy as well.

He was not. He said she was lying, then denied being the father, accused her of sleeping around and swore he would never marry her anyway. "Get serious," he said "just look at yourself!" He gave her a look of contempt and shut the door in her face. She stood there for a while, shocked, hurt and feeling helpless.

This was a time when choices were few for women in her condition and a girl would only be faced with shame and scorn no matter what she did. This was a time when a man could lie to a woman and never be held accountable for his wondering sperm. Pat was scared and alone. She slowly walked back home, using a headache as an excuse to stay away from the dinner table and avoid any conversation.

That fateful morning, her sister came down to breakfast and, seeing Pat looking forlorn and haggard, asked what the hell was wrong with her. Shelly was tall and built like one imagines a farm girl should be. She was already past what was considered 'marrying age' and had no time for romance, sappy movies or dating. She ran the house, helped with the animals, all efficiently and with only pleasing her father as a goal.

Pat had never been close to her sister, apart from having to share a bedroom, but after the night she had just lived through, she hoped Shelly would pretend to be her mom and help her out. She broke down and confided in her only sibling. She was convinced that as a woman, Shelly would understand her predicament.

Instead, her sister had become very angry, waking her dad and then both wanting to know how, when it had happened, and whose bastard it was. Pat felt degraded and humiliated without being given a chance to explain. She had been in love. He was going to marry her, he said. She just sobbed quietly with her head hanging in shame.

There was no doubt in her dad's mind that Pat would have to leave. Still crying, she climbed the stairs to her room, packed a small bag and walked out. She had a bit of money from odd jobs after school, so she walked to town and tried to remember another girl who had found herself in the same predicament. A name finally came to mind and she went to the diner where she knew she would find her. The young woman now worked as a waitress; she was a former classmate who had dropped out last year after finding she was pregnant. She never had the baby, but the damage was done and her former friends turned their heads whenever they saw her.

She gave Pat a name and address where she could get rid of the baby at a good price. She also offered to put her up until Pat got a job and found a place of her own. At first, it seemed that all had gone well until the bleeding started and Pat found out that the price of this abortion also included giving up any hope of ever bearing any children.

She never returned home. She found a job in town as a receptionist in a law firm, a room in a boarding house, and was encouraged by her new employer to study and get a legal assistant certificate.

As soon as she had saved enough money, she moved as far as she could from her roots hoping she could forget this life ever existed.

As a serious applicant with good experience, Pat quickly found work in her new town. It was at the law firm where she met Bill. End of story.

She later made a feeble attempt to communicate with her family sending her father and sister a wedding invitation. The only response was from Shelly, telling her of their father's death from liver failure the previous year and how she now was running the farm by herself and had no time for frivolities like weddings. So, apart from some colleagues from work, there was no one to make theirs a family wedding.

Pat tried to hide her disappointment and made no further effort to communicate with her sister. Ten years later, a probate attorney who had searched for her, informed her that Shelly had died and, as the sole survivor of the family, the small homestead was now hers.

She continued paying the taxes and whatever utilities had to be maintained for all these years but never visited, rented or even considered selling the property. Bill was aware of the inheritance but knew not to ask any questions.

##

That is where Pat was going now. The anger she had been harboring most of her young adult life had been re-ignited and she needed to close some gaps and understand what lies between the past and her future.

With Bill as a steady mate, one who made no demands on her, Pat had managed to resist any remote idea of closure. He had been her rock and had protected her from anything disturbing or that would distract her from the daily routine they both enjoyed.

She had never confided in Bill about the abortion. He never asked about her past, she never told. This was between her and her conscience which was clear. She had no options at the time. It was the right thing to do. Until yesterday, Pat had always thought Bill had no place in his life for children, but she sometimes wondered why he had never brought up that subject. Now she knew.

The sun was now setting, blinding her every time she rounded a curve. It was huge, orange and reminiscent of those old fashion 'walking into the sunset' oaters.

The names on the exit signs started looking more and more familiar. There was no interstate the last time she was here, so she'd have to look for some landmark to guide her, in case the small town was now unmarked and unnoticeable. Pat had not kept up with what was happening in this part of the country which she had deemed dead to her forever.

By the time she rolled into town it was dark and most streets were deserted. She had been surprised to find that her hometown not only had its own exit ramp, but now boasted a branch of the State University and all the chain restaurants and department stores found all over the country.

Not knowing what kind of shape the house was in, she decided to stay at a motel close to the interstate for the night. Her room faced the parking lot, but she could still hear the trucks speeding on the highway. A thunderstorm also raged all night to seal a sleepless one for this prodigal child. Rain was still falling in the morning when Pat stopped at a fast food place for breakfast and set out to recapture her past.

The ride to the farm was met with patches of fog and slick pavement. The town had developed along the highway. The expansion had not reached this county road which was still lined with farms and trailers where farmhands were housed in the summer. Pat stopped in front of her childhood home. It had not changed at all. The white paint was peeling in places and the tin roof showed breaks and missing pieces, but this is how it had looked the last time Pat had seen it.

The gravel driveway was now mostly mud but she managed to drive into the car port next to the house. Visions of rats, spiders and mice, even perhaps raccoons, flashed in front of her mind's eye. She sighed, turned the ignition off and got out of the car.

She had received keys along with the property's information, and wondered if they would still work. To her surprise, the door opened easily. Walking into the farmhouse however, was a shock. Her nostrils were attacked by a musty scent of mildew mixed with dust and the odor stale air acquires over the years. She left the door opened but knew that with water logged ground and the rain still falling, it would be a while before fresh air could penetrate this house.

She sneezed, blew her nose and looked around, taking in the changes in the hallway. The flowered paper in the hall was gone. The walls were all painted some neutral tone. Her mother's touch had been completely obliterated.

The living room furniture was different as well. Large upholstered sectional sofas and a glass coffee table replaced the couch and small chairs next to lace covered rosewood tables she remembered from her childhood. There were no family pictures on the wall, not that there ever had been, but she would have liked to see if Shelly and her father's lives had gone through significant events while she was gone. The shag carpet was worn and, together with the sofas, showed signs of mildew and wear from years of neglect.

The dining room was the same as she remembered: no one had ever used it while she was growing up. No one seemed to have used it since. It reminded her more of her grandparents from whom the dining room set had been inherited and kept more as a relic than something to be used by the family.

The ceiling, sagging over the water stained serving table, threatened to collapse at any time. The door to the kitchen had been closed from the hallway and the swing door from this room was closed as well. She pushed it open. The small fifties' style refrigerator and stove were gone and had made room for brown colored appliances of no significance. The yellow table with chrome edges had been replaced by a corner bench and a melamine table unit. No one had bothered to change the old linoleum floor which showed wear and the faint hint of a pattern which Pat remembered as large green flowers.

She could see that weeds and wild flowers had replaced the kitchen garden Shelly used to tend in the back yard and the look was that of abandon. The deep ruts and paths from her dad's trucks and tractor that ran from the house to the barn had long been covered by weeds and shrubs.

Pat thought of sitting there to regain some sense of home, but the chairs, the table, the entire décor was so foreign; it did not stir any memories or give her a sense of familiarity.

She made her way back to the front. The third step creaked as she was climbing up to see the bedrooms just as it had done those thirty years ago. To the right had been her parents' room. She only opened the door enough to glimpse into what used to be a sacrosanct refuge away from her and her sister. Pat had always been intimidated by that room and was now wondering if she ever even had entered that space. It looked familiar, but her only mental note was that she thought it was so much larger at the time.

The door to the bathroom facing the stairs was open and showed no sign of renovations. Pat went in and flushed to see if the plumbing was working. The yellowed porcelain toilet responded dutifully and Pat thought amazing how bathroom technology had not changed much in the half century since she was born.

To the left was the bedroom she and Shelly shared. She hesitated and walked in. The beds were still against opposite walls; nothing looked as if the occupants had been gone, one for over thirty years, the other for ten.

She sat at the small vanity which consisted of a slab of wood, painted white and trimmed with blue tulle fabric held together by thumbtacks. Over the table on the wall was a frilly, round mirror where she used to stare at herself, elbows on the table, wondering what she had done to God to deserve the long nose, the wide, cow-like eyes and a hint of a double chin in spite of her skinny shapeless body. Pat looked up and saw that child in the mirror, only older, sadder and alone.

So far Pat had seen no vermin and for that she was grateful. A familiar noise brought her back to the past: the roof over the closet leaked. Can this be the same leak or, the same roof? She walked over and peered in the closet to find that after all this time, the floor had allowed the rain to rot through the wood and, Pat assumed, all the way through where the ceiling was threatening to fall over the dining room. She also saw that the few clothes she had owned were still hanging and her old farm boots were rooted to the floor, home to probably a hundred spiders.

This room was the same as when she had left it. This is where she had to be if any feelings were to return and if she was to make peace with her childhood.

She looked at the window to see the same sheer curtains with pales lilac flowers let the light in. She peaked through, noticed a crack near the upper sill, and found that the rain had stopped.

From the lack of personal effects in that room, she assumed her sister had taken over the master bedroom after her dad died and this is where she would have to look for answers.

Pat was a practical woman. In spite of trying to have some emotional reaction to this house, she was mentally making a list of all the repairs she would have to make, even if she decided to sell it. What should she do next? So far, nothing hurt, nothing felt good and she wasn't ready to dig any deeper into the past.

She walked back downstairs and hoped to find at least some basic electrical appliances working. Staying here tonight would surely bring the ghosts back. She wanted ghosts, she needed ghosts.

She first looked for the fuse box and was pleased to see that it had been updated to circuit breakers after she had gone. Knowing she never had the electricity disconnected, she reset all the switches and crossed her fingers. A light came on in the kitchen. A good sign.

She meandered around, turned lights off and on, some with success most without and eventually found that what used to be a wood shed had been transformed into a laundry room. The appliances showed signs of rust at the bottom, but, checking on the water and electrical connections, she twisted the knob, and brownish, yellow, gritty water came out.

She went outside through the back door which protested and stuck to the pane until Pat gave it a swift kick. There was no back porch anymore. It had rotted away and grass was growing through what had been wooden planks and a railing. She carefully made her way to the barn, aware but unconcerned with the mud now crawling onto her old running shoes. The door was slightly ajar and she saw from the number of beer cans, bottles and empty cigarette packs, that some neighborhood kids had used the premises to hold drinking parties. She was surprised but grateful that they had left the house alone.

The tractor had been vandalized and rusted pieces of it were scattered throughout the barn. The family farm was not a rich one, so there had been little else in the barn. She had told the attorney to sell her sister's car, and, in retrospect, she should have included the farm equipment as well. The smell of moldy hay and urine chased her out and she took in the field which had been where she had hid so often as a child, waiting for someone to find her.

There were ten acres left from the original hundred which had to be shared by ten siblings when her dad's parents had died before she was born. Most had sold their land and moved on. Her parents couldn't afford buying them off so they had continued growing corn on six of the acres. They also used half an acre to grow vegetables which they sold at the town market from June to October on Saturday mornings.

The whole place was overgrown with plants and shrubs seeded by birds over the years. The chicken coop still remained on the other side of the house, now vacant for many years. Pat remembered omelets made from eggs freshly collected from the hen and smiled at the memory.

By the time she became aware of passing time, Pat realized lunch had come and gone and she would have to do some work if she was going to move in today. She walked back to the house, carefully taking her shoes off in spite of the already dirty linoleum, checked the refrigerator, found it inoperable, and started on a list of absolute necessities at least for the first night.

Two hours and another meal at the fast food restaurant later, Pat was back with some basic supplies: new light bulbs, soap, towel, paper, a good sleeping bag as well as basic food and drink supplies which would take care of the first night and tomorrow morning. She didn't know how long she would be here, so she postponed any more efforts towards making the house livable.

Her first stop was the master bedroom. She cleaned the lamp socket after painstakingly and carefully removing the rusty light bulb, crossed her finger, screwed a new bulb in and, yes, it worked. Encouraged by this effort, Pat wondered around the house and found home for the other five bulbs she had purchased. She then put the sleeping bag on her old bed, ready to be used in case sleepiness took over and she had no more strength to set it up.

Pat and Bill had never been ones to drink, but she had made sure a bottle of wine was on the list of supplies. She needed something to loosen her mind and allow the ghosts to seep in. Daylight was fading as she was making a nest for herself and finally went downstairs to open the bottle of wine. She had never thought of purchasing a corkscrew and was pleased if not surprised to find one in a kitchen drawer.

She could think of no reason to procrastinate any longer. She climbed the stairs again and found her way to the master bedroom. She knew her parents, and then apparently her sister, kept records for the farm, the house and their personal business in a small desk under the window facing the back yard. The curtain was opened, unmoved for the last ten years.

She looked out; all was dark by then. Pat tried to picture how the farm had looked when she was still living here. She couldn't. She shrugged and concentrated on the goal she had set for herself on this first night back.

Opening one of the left drawers, she found ledgers after ledgers, carefully filled out with columns of information on crops, amount of sales, all in her sister's small precise handwriting, or 'chicken scratch' as her dad used to call it.

The bottom one was filled with pictures. Pat remembered the 5 and 10 and its photo booth where she would run to with her sister when her dad gave them the 25 cents to get four thumbnail size pictures.

There were also state fair and occasional school photos, but nothing to show what had happened after she left.

She opened the middle drawer and saw papers, strewn about, in no particular order. After coming across copies of letters written to utility companies or complaining about credit issues, Pat found what she knew she was looking for.

"Dear Shelley,

I am sorry about your father and regret that you can't attend our wedding. I also appreciate your writing to me and informing me of Patricia's childhood indiscretion. However, I'll have you know that this will affect in no way my decision to marry your sister, a most intelligent, sensitive and lovely woman as I have ever met.

She never mentioned the awful stories you related to me in your letter. I will not confront or even ask about its veracity since we all have things we wish we could take back, and I'm sure it is not my concern in any case. Most of us move on from our mistakes and look for new ways to fulfill our lives.

I would very much appreciate your never communicating with either one of us as I intend to make Patricia happy in spite of the family she cannot count on. I love and respect her and know she trusts me to accept her as she is and I do.

With all due respect, I don't understand how you found it in your heart to write to me, slandering my fiancée and jeopardizing your own sister's happiness. You must be a very bitter woman and I feel sorry for you.

I look forward to our wedding day and while you found it necessary to tell me that here will be no children from our marriage, I also know we will be very happy as long as you stay out of our lives.

Sincerely,
Bill"

Pat's tears were already dropping on the letter. She held it against her heart, turned the lamp off and walked back into her own room. She continued sobbing for a long time, the first time in months.

She had been terrified after finding her sister's correspondence in Bill private file from work. Shelly had described her sister in such a foul language and with such venom, Pat was afraid to find out what had been Bill's reaction. She knew there would be a letter and she was hoping to find it; he may have been a simple man but he would never let something like this go. She just was terrified of what it contained. Did he marry her out of pity? Was he so desperate that he went through the marriage in spite of knowing her secret?

She would have liked to know how her sister had found out about her botched abortion and how long she had held this information in reserve to try and ruin any chance of happiness she could have. But there would be time for this later. It all didn't have to happen tonight.

Bill's spirit was now in the room with her. He filled her heart with such love and his presence was so real, she could feel him smile at her from the door. She sat once again in front of the vanity and this time, when she looked up at the woman she was now, she only saw the aura of Bill's love surrounding her face. She could finally come home.

She would be fifty years old tomorrow and the ghosts were all gone save for Bill's lingering spirit. Maybe she would paper the wall again with flowers to get her mother's back.

##

www.ingramcontent.com/pod-product-compliance
Lightning Source LLC
Chambersburg PA
CBHW060422030726
47495CB00003B/689